330 LOVE LN.

A CHERRY FALLS ROMANCE

MIKA JOLIE

1

MILLIE

A woman can get through anything with a little T. Swift.

It's a fact of life.

One I embrace every chance I get, but especially at lunch when I jam out eating my crunchy peanut butter and strawberry jelly sandwich. I would have gone over to Virgin Street Diner, where my brother David works as a line cook, for a grilled cheese, but he kept grumbling about another worker making eyes at me. A sweet, sixteen-year-old kid who needs a dermatologist more than a date.

Despite the half-eaten sandwich, and the tunes blaring through my wireless earbuds, I'm restless. My skin feels too tight over my bones, and it's a little harder to keep myself contained today. As if I might float away on the cedar-scented breeze that washes through the shop when Rueben, my other brother, leaves the doors propped open.

I sing along with the lyrics. Something about a great escape and a prison break. Something I can relate to. I live in Cherry Falls, a small town with few people, who all know each other.

Today is a beautiful spring day in late March. The winter time has passed in its somber majesty. There's a little crowd in town as it is a bright and sunny afternoon. On the right side of town is a lumber and hardware store that my family owns. Harper Lumber Co., my father called it, and he worked there day and night with my mom. It was their accomplishment, their pride and joy, and that and the house were the only tangible things in their will.

The problem is, I long to get out of this tiny town and pursue my dream of becoming a singer, but my older brothers are against it, so I take the hardware store as my stage.

I reach the end and hum the notes since the words don't come to me. Then I pop a blueberry in my mouth and rock my head to the beat. Taylor Swift always has a way of making me feel safe with whatever I'm feeling. She's been my lifeline growing up with two overly protective older brothers.

A hand lands hard on my shoulder, and I nearly jump out of the chair. Tugging the earbuds from my ears, I look up at Rueben. Ten years older than me, with the same mahogany brown hair, although his is threaded with tiny hints of silver as he towers over my compact frame.

"You doin' okay?" he asks in that all knowing older brother tone.

I nod and set my earbuds on the table next to the remains of my lunch. "Sure, just taking my break. How are you?"

He studies me, and I try not to squirm under the scrutiny.

I fail and tug the ends of my midnight blue shirt over my wrists. "Did you need me to help a customer?"

"Nah. About this weekend...we should visit Mom and Dad."

A surge of pain wells up inside me. The anniversary of their death is approaching. Thirteen years since they've been gone. Their lives cut short by a drunk driver. The thoughts of them have become stronger over the years. At times I've pushed them back, sought even to extinguish them. I know this is only a reaction to the pain of their absence. In truth, I wish they were here, especially for days like today when all I want to do is pack my bag and pursue my dreams, for better or worse.

God, my heart hurts.

With a grunt, he lowers himself into the chair next to mine. "Was that a new Swifty song? You sound better than she does, in my opinion."

I can't stop the laugh which cracks out of me. "Sure, yeah. Changing the subject. What's up?"

Only then do I notice his uncomfortable lean toward me. The grimace on his tan face. The same expression he had the time I had to explain—in detail—which brand of tampons I needed from the grocery store.

"You've got that look—like you swallowed too much water at once, and you're not sure if it ended up in your belly or your lungs."

He snorts. "I was just thinking maybe we should go to the diner for dinner. Bug David for a bit, remind him we're here."

"He knows we're here. Were you not at dinner with him at our house last night?"

"I just—"

I put my hand on his arm, which rests between us on the table. "Spit it out. What's wrong? I can't fix it if I don't know what the problem is."

"I worry about when David is going to leave again. He said he'd stay for a while this time, but I fear he's getting restless. I need you both here with me so I can keep you safe."

Both of my brothers have a heart of gold. I understand where Rueben is coming from. After our parents' accident, David took over the store for a while. A couple of years ago, he fell in love, got married, and moved to Syn City, leaving Rueben and I in charge of the shop. We were okay with the decision. At the end of the day, we wanted our brother to be happy. Unfortunately, the marriage didn't last and since then David has been traveling on his motorcycle. Cherry Falls is a pit stop. I'm just happy he's back...even if it's for a little while.

With a small smile, I rub Rueben's arm with my hand. "He's your big brother, isn't he the one meant to keep you safe?"

He captures my hand in his own calloused ones. "Not with that death trap of a motorcycle he can't. I worry about him every day, out there on the road, and back here. I worry that being stuck here is killing him slowly. And I worry if he leaves, it'll kill me slowly."

This is the most about his feelings my brother has shared with me in a very long time. I try not to move, hoping he'll keep telling me what he's thinking. But he lapses into silence and stares off toward the lumber piles in the back of the warehouse.

Guilt pours through me as I remember, only moments ago, I contemplated what it would be like to leave this place for a while. Seek out a new dream. It's only a fantasy— something to pass the days, get me through the nights. I could never leave him, not after everything Rueben and David have done for me. Not after they raised me after our parents died when they could have shipped me off to a relative.

"Do you think we can talk him into coming back to work here? If he's around more often, maybe I can wear him down," Rueben muses.

I give his hand a squeeze and shake my head. "Not without a serious reason. He likes his independence. And he doesn't want us getting used to relying on him in case he runs off at the drop of a hat." *Like last time.*

He nods, tugs his hands back, and stands. "You're right. But I'm still going to try and convince him. Maybe we should bring back family game night? Or family bowling on Wednesdays? What do you think?"

As gently as I can, I tell him. "If David doesn't want to stay, I don't think any amount of Monopoly, or half-priced games at Holidaze Arcade and Bar, is going to convince him." I say, naming the old school arcade in Kissme Bay, the next town over.

He blinks and nods. "No, you're right, of course. Well, let's start with dinner and see what we can do between us. You'll help me, right? Convince him he should stay here with us for a while?"

A tight fist constricts around my heart. I wish I could leave too, see the world through my eyes rather than through the stories David tells me.

Another wave of guilt assails me. How could I talk David into staying when I can barely talk myself into it? It's getting harder and harder the more time passes. The more social media stars I see turning their dreams into reality. But there's no other choice. Not when Rueben asks me for something.

"Of course, I'll help." I force fake cheer into my tone. "Just tell me what you need, and I'll do my best. Even if it means pretending to lose every game on bowling night so he can spend the rest of his days in town a winner."

That statement earns me a smile and a nod of approval. I used to long for those moments. I know he's proud of me, he's always told me that, but it's different now, as an adult. Earning his approval as a child was a given. As a twenty-four-year-old woman...sometimes I'm not sure that I still need it.

The alarm on my phone blares, startling us both. With a laugh, I shove off the table, pack up the rest of my lunch, except for the few blueberries in the small plastic tray, and tuck my earbuds into my pocket. "Time to get back to work."

Rueben pushes up the heavy rolling door on the far end of the shop to the warehouse, creating a nice cross breeze between the back and front doors. My hair flies around my face in the wind as I tuck the last of the blueberries into my palm and head back toward the main retail area. It's been a slow morning, and I don't expect a huge rush of customers, but I prefer to be ready if they do show up. Besides, it keeps me busy, and if I do get a customer, it will drag me out of my own head for a while.

Rueben needs me. David is only here because of us. I can't possibly leave them, especially to pursue a dream which has little chance of succeeding. After our parents' untimely death, they took custody of me, took care of me, when they were only in their early twenties. My brothers have always supported me. Taking me to voice and piano lessons as a teenager, working longer hours to pay for it all. Now, when they need me here most, I can't abandon them to chase a child's fantasy.

"Yeah, go to work, slacker, I'm going to take a nap," Rueben calls as he heads to our office above the warehouse space.

I glance back at him, my melancholy thoughts fleeing, and shake my head. Then I run smack into a wall of... muscle? Not solid muscle like some of the bodybuilders in town, but long lean graceful muscles. Like a swimmer or a runner possesses.

With his wide chest so prominently in front of my face, it takes me a moment to orient myself. It's attached to a tall man, with a long, graceful neck and eyes the color of rich black walnut wood. His short hair is a darker shade than mine.

Time stops between us, as if it's holding its breath. No, that's just me. His hand steadies my arm, and I jerk back to the present, heat already washing into my neck and ears.

Then I realize when I stumbled, I squeezed the blueberries into a pulp, which is now spread across his clean white shirt.

The heat's burning across my ears now. No doubt staining my cheeks in a blush of epic proportions. "Oh my goodness. I'm so sorry."

As if drawn from his own reverie, he glances down at the mess on his shirt. "Oh, well. I guess it's a good thing I need to head home and change."

I dash to the counter and tug out several clean rags we keep there for dusting and race back to him. He watches as my gaze bounces between the already setting stain and his amused expression.

"Let me help."

After a minute of scrubbing, my own palm now stained with the telltale purplish-blue, he stills my fingers beneath his own. "Please, it's fine. This is an old shirt, anyway. No harm done."

"But..."

He shakes his head gently and gives me a full smile.

Gleaming white teeth and plush lips strike me stupid as I stare at him. "I'm fine. The shirt is going in the washing machine when I get home. It's all good."

Then his eyes take on a new gleam. "You look familiar to me somehow. Have we met before?"

I almost want to laugh. As if I wouldn't remember meeting this beautiful man. "No, I'm sorry, I don't think so. Was there something I can help you with?" I stare at the blueberry streak. It's almost mocking me with its vivid hue. "I'll happily buy you a new shirt if you can't get that stain out."

Rueben, of course, makes the perfect entrance, clearing his throat behind me. "Can I help you?"

The man stares down at me for another beat before shifting his gaze to my brother, who no doubt scowls at the proximity the stranger and I share.

I step away so he can approach my brother, and when he steals a glance back at me, I take off toward the front counter, as far away from him, and my mortification, as I can manage.

2

———

TYLER

The studio door is unlocked. Relief washes through me as the gentle strains of someone tuning a guitar reach me. For a second, I had flashbacks of when Cash, our bassist, left our van unlocked one time and our backup equipment got stolen.

I close and lock the door behind me. Grateful all over again that we aren't begging friends to let us play in their garages and basements anymore. We splurged on a studio last year with the help of our part-time manager, Clint. And I don't think we'd ever be able to go back to the way it was before. It was terrible trying to fit in practice for four people, all our gear, within the other person's availability to let us use their space.

Coby Rae—our kick ass drummer and the only female in the band—sits behind her drums, the sticks stuck through the massive top knot her long hair makes at the crown of her head. Her brown eyes cut to mine the moment I come into view. "You're late."

I shrug and gesture at the blue stain on my shirt. "Had an incident. But don't worry, the blueberries had it coming."

She rolls her eyes at my joke but doesn't comment.

Gavin, our guitarist, lays sprawled sideways on the ratty armchair Cash found in an alley when we first took over the studio. His long hair lays in a mass of black glossy curls almost to the floor. There's a dark edge to him; it's been there since we first met. The scowl on his face and the perpetual black of his wardrobe is a clear indication today is no different.

As usual, he says nothing when I enter nor when I perch on the edge of the stool situated in front of my microphone.

Cash, bass in hand, gently strums the strings as he tunes his instrument. His brown hair is long on top, slicked back, and shaved on the sides. He always gets shit for not being in a heavy metal band with his look. But the ladies seem to love all the tattoos and the southern drawl he wields against them to great effect.

My mind flashes back to the girl in the hardware store and the wide-eyed gape she'd given me. I get looks like that on stage every time we play, but it felt different coming from her. Those vivid green eyes meeting mine, I think she actually blushed. It was damn cute.

I shift on the stool and face them. "Do we want to practice today?"

We need to since we have a gig coming up, but even my mind isn't on the music. It's back at that store. Wondering what her name is and if her long brown hair is as soft as it looked.

Coby striking her crash cymbal makes me jump out of my skin and we all glare at her.

"What? You were late. I wanted to practice earlier, but now I'm not in the mood. Why don't we just go over the set list instead?"

I wave at her. "Go for it."

She leans forward on her stool and drags a folded-up piece of notebook paper from her ripped jeans pocket. "As agreed, we've cut the last of our covers, and now we're on an entirely original list. Everyone still good with baring our souls to a crowd of drunken strangers?"

Cash and Gavin grumble their assent, and I simply nod. "Are you? We were all in agreement before."

She reads over the list one more time and then tosses the paper onto her snare. "Yeah. I'm good." Her tone isn't convincing, though.

I share a look with Cash, who ducks his chin to frown into his strings as if he needs their emotional support to deal with his recalcitrant bandmate.

"Well, we all know the set by now. If we aren't going to practice, should we talk about Clint's calendar? He sent it out in a group email, but I feel like he could branch out for us more."

Gavin pipes up, still sideways on his chair. "You want to go on tour, dude?"

"No, it's not like I want to go out on the road or anything, but I'd prefer more clubs to college bar gigs. Something that pays and gets us more of a following."

Cash puts his bass on the stand and shifts on his own stool. "They're the same places he's been sending us to since he took the job as our part-time manager—the non-paying part-time manager position. If we get demanding, we might have to find someone who actually manages people for a living."

I shrug, squaring my shoulders, for the fight sure to come. "And why is that a bad thing? If we want to grow, we need to find someone who has our growth in mind."

Gavin swings his legs down and sits up, his hair falling over his shoulder as he levels his dark brown eyes at me. "We—"

My phone rings loudly, echoing throughout the room, and I dig it out of my pocket. Only one person ever calls me, and I always answer for him.

I hold up my hand and press the phone to my ear. "Hey, Gramps. What's up? I'm at practice, so I only have a minute to talk."

Gramps' deep baritone cuts through the line, making me smile. "Oh, I'm just callin' to see how you are and to ask if you're going with me this weekend?"

I shuffle off toward the windows that face the street. "Going where?"

"To Baker City."

I remain silent on the other end. Baker City, Oregon, is my hometown, where I was born and raised up until I was about thirteen...until my parents' car accident that ended their lives. After that, my mother's father took custody of me. From that time on we've been living in Rosewood Ranch Lands.

"Well, you know, " Gramps starts again, "it's almost the anniv—"

I cut him off. "Ah, Gramps, can we talk about this later? I'm going to be there for dinner, and we can discuss everything."

Gramps sighs, and a twinge of guilt works its way into my chest. The man raised me, and I want to give him everything, show him how much I appreciate him. But talking about the anniversary of my parents' death isn't high on my to do list right now.

"Dinner then. I'll make fish," Gramps says.

I can't help but smile at that. He always cooks fish. "See you then."

We hang up, and I swing around to face the group, ready for the argument, but they seem to have moved on and are heatedly going back and forth about the song order.

I'm happy they are getting into it, though. This change is a year in the making. Covers were great for us years ago when Devil on the Highway first got its sea legs. Now, we'd built a following. A local following, but still, we're earning enough for the band to be our full time job. And if people come to our gigs, I want them to hear *us*, not just the artists we cover.

I plop back on the stool and listen to them go back and forth about the sequence of our songs. It doesn't matter to me what order they're in. I'm just excited to be playing them at all.

When Coby seems satisfied, she makes a last flourish on the sheet with a red pen she unearthed from her bun and hands it to me. "What do you think of that?"

Gavin gathers his curls into a ponytail, shoves out of the chair, crosses the room to the mini fridge and pulls out some drinks. He passes beers to Coby and Gavin, then hands me a water, and takes his own beer back to his chair.

I hug the cool water bottle to my chest and review the set list but barely register any changes. I'll memorize it the day of the show like I always do. If I get too into my head about it, it throws me off.

So, I nod. "Looks great."

The girl at the store pops back into my head. What would she look like standing in the crowd dancing to my music? Dancing to my songs? I like the image more than I probably should.

I take a minute and fiddle with the cords on my microphone. Then remember I'd gone to the hardware store to get zip ties but forgot with the entire run-in and then ensuing blueberry mishap.

It would mean I'd have to go back. A smile spreads across my face before I can reel it back in.

"What's that look for?" Coby asks.

I shake my head. "Nothing, just thinking about the show. It's going to be great. We're all going to be great."

Cash narrows his eyes at me but goes back to his guitar. Of the group, he's always been the person I've felt closest to. No doubt he can smell my bullshit from across the room.

I change the subject. "Anyway, so no practice. Dinner at the usual time for the pre-show ritual?"

It's Coby's turn to glare. "Obviously. Unless you want to change that too."

She's five feet of attitude, always ready to ignite. It's what we all love about her, and why she makes such a damn talented drummer. Change has always been hard for her, and every time she lashes out verbally, it's her way of asking for reassurance. For us men, it took way too long to learn that lesson.

"French toast, two sides of bacon extra crispy for the angry drummer," I say.

Everyone laughs, even Coby. The tension disappears, and the guys start packing up their guitars. I leave my set up in place as I don't need it to practice at home.

Coby also leaves her instruments behind. She keeps an electronic set up back at the apartment she shares with Gavin. They both needed a place after they got out of school, and somehow her high strung personality doesn't clash with the dark, brooding edges of his. They've been roommates for a couple of years and seem content. I still think one day they'll kill each other.

I give my friends a salute. "Great practice, everyone."

Coby groans at my sarcasm and shoves me out ahead of her. Smiling, I duck away and head toward the door. My mind already back at the hardware store.

3

____

MILLIE

The store is quiet, just like I prefer it. Sure, when we're busy, we make a lot more money, but sometimes, I love the breeze rolling through the warehouse, and the soft chime of wrenches swaying against each other on their displays.

I've got my earbuds in, a song on low, more for background noise than anything, while I dust the shelves behind the counter. Rueben hates doing it, and I don't think David even knows we own a duster, so it's often left to me. Not that I mind. Technically, David doesn't work here anymore, and the work makes me feel useful.

I'm happily dusting and humming along with Dolly Parton as she sings "Jolene". In my mind, I'm on stage, and the noise is blaring as I let the lyrics carry me over. Somewhere in the recess of my mind, I hear the chime of the front doorbell. I stop and whirl around, a pleasant smile already in place, and I come face to face with the man I accosted with my blueberries the other day.

Dang, I thought I imagined him to be so good looking.

He smiles as he approaches the counter, grey t-shirt hugging solid muscles as he bellies up to the edge. "Hi."

"Hi," I stammer out, jerking my earbuds out of my ears and resting them on the counter.

He narrows his eyes and drags one toward him, then holds it to his ear and taps it to turn the music back on. The strains of the song start up again, and he smiles. Dimples dig grooves into his handsome cheeks. "I love this one. It's a classic."

When I just stare, he returns my earbud, and I quickly shove them into my jeans pocket and wipe my hands on the denim for good measure. No doubt dust clings to them, and to the peony shirt I'd chosen to brighten up my day. "Um, give me a minute and someone will be up to help you."

I try to flee to the back, but he catches my wrist gently with his hand. "Please, all I need is a second. I just came to tell you my shirt made it through unscathed."

Psh. Now who's making things up? I gently tug my wrist free and put my hands on my hips. My friend, Jess, calls it my Wonder Woman pose, the position I take when I'm trying to put a little authority in my tone. Too bad it doesn't work on my brothers. "Well, I think that's a lie, but it's sweet all the same."

He ducks his head and a wash of pink stains his cheeks. I'm gaping at him again. Did I actually inspire a blush? "Okay, you're right, I lied, but only because I didn't want you to feel bad. But please, don't worry about it, I have plenty of shirts, and I don't need you to buy me another one. I really just wanted an excuse to come by here, to see you again, well besides to get the zip ties I forgot the last time."

"An excuse to see me?" I try to keep the fact that I'm dumbfounded out of my tone.

That dang smile again. "Of course. I didn't get your name last time. I'm Tyler Yates."

"Millie Cantal. What did you need me to help you with?"

He laughs this time, a sound that releases butterflies in my chest. "I came to ask if you wanted to come to a concert. My band is playing at Fireside Bar and Grill, tonight, and maybe you'd want to come watch? I can get you and a friend in for free...as long as it's not a male friend." He throws in a wink, and I snort.

I grab a bag of zip ties off one of the shelves and hand it to him. "I don't get out to concerts much. What's your band's name?" I ask as we head back to the cash register.

Leaning on the counter, he seems to settle in. "Devil on the Highway. Have you heard of us?"

I shake my head and gesture at the earbuds. "No, sorry."

He drags his hand to his heart and gasps. "That's a damn shame. Well, come tonight, and we can broaden your horizons."

The way he said that made it sound way more intimate than a crowded bar. "I don't know. It'll depend on if I can get away or not."

"Of course. No pressure. I'd love to see you, though. You have a beautiful voice. A singer?"

"No." I ring his purchase. As he hands me the payment our fingers brush. Once again I'm thrown in a trance and meet his gaze. Sexual tension hangs heavy in the air, which is weird to me. I don't know this guy, and neither does he know me, but the way we are together right now is steamy, a little uncomfortable, but I don't mind getting comfortable with discomfort.

Rueben stalks into the room, and I freeze as if I was trying to rob a bank and was caught in the act.

"See what now?" he asks, staring between us expectantly.

Tyler straightens himself to his full height. "I was just inviting Millie to come to my concert tonight."

"She's busy."

Tyler glances over at me. "I think she can speak for herself."

I mouth to him. "Sorry."

Instead of replying, Rueben holds Tyler's stare, who shockingly doesn't flinch. After a few seconds, which feel like hours, Tyler turns to me again. "Hope to see you there."

"Umm, let me get you the zip ties." I hand him the small bag.

"Thanks." He gives me a brief nod and saunters out the door like my brother didn't just force him out with the power of his short sightedness.

Once Tyler is gone, I round on Rueben and rush around the counter. "What is your problem?"

"My problem? You were just out here flirting."

I don't bother to hide the outrage no doubt stamped on my face. "Are you kidding me? He came here to invite me to a concert, not an orgy."

He jabs his finger toward the door. "Guys only want one thing from pretty girls. They want to get into their pants."

I'm super done with this conversation. Untying my green apron from around my waist, I shove it at his chest. "I can't believe you just said that to me. I'm not a little girl anymore. And if a man wants to get into my pants, that is none of your, or David's, business. I'll unbutton my pants for anyone I want."

As I stalk out of the back door and head toward my car, I know my tirade didn't come out as planned, but the sentiment stands. Rueben and David have been scaring off my dates for years. It's the big reason I'm still a virgin at twenty-four. Not that I would tell them that, or they'd only lock down my world tighter knowing their antics work.

When I turn the ignition in my car, it sputters, and I smack the steering wheel. "Come on!" Another two tries brings the old engine back to life, and I peel out of the parking lot. Technically, I'm not supposed to leave until lunch, but I've had about enough of seeing Rueben's face for one morning.

I put my earbud back in, connect it to my phone, and call my best friend, Jess.

She answers on the second ring. "What's up? I thought you didn't get off until later?"

"I decided I needed to take a personal day. Have you heard of a band called Devil on the Highway? Apparently, they're playing at the tavern tonight, and I was thinking about going."

Her excited squeal forces me to remove my earbud for a moment. When she settles, I shove it back in.

"Of course, I love that band. Can I come?"

I chuckle. "Of course. I need help with an outfit and someone to watch my drinks when I go to the restroom."

"Obviously the job of every good wing woman. Pick me up later, and I'll have the outfits ready."

4

____

MILLIE

I should have rethought giving Jess free rein over my wardrobe tonight. The short jean mini skirt isn't something I would usually wear, and the black tank top rides up to show my belly as I dance, leaving me constantly tugging it down.

She's in a rainbow sequin halter dress, her blond corkscrew curls a riot around her face. Fireside Bar and Grill is packed, and the band is good. We've taken up a position in the crowd near the stage for the best view. I can't stop staring at Tyler every time he steps up to the mic. He swirls with positive energy that I find attractive.

A bar sits in the corner, TVs suspended above it, but no one lingers there. Not a soul in this place can take their eyes off Tyler and the band. He owns the place and everyone in it.

When the music softens, and he shifts into a ballad, I can't help but feel like he sings every word for me. Especially, when he locks eyes with me again, as he's done all night. I'm so amped from his attention, my fingers and toes tingle.

The crowd is winding down, and I'm worried I won't get a chance to talk to him before I have to haul Jess back to her place. But then he turns to the band and whispers something to them. They all nod except the drummer who seems to glare at Tyler, but she resettles on her stool, anyway.

His lovely deep voice calls to the crowd. "I want to invite a friend up here on stage. She reminded me how much I love this song today, so I want to sing it for you now as our last number. And I'm going to need a little help."

I glance around uncertainly until he hops off stage and makes a beeline straight for me.

Oh. Oh no.

"Come on, sing with me."

I shake my head frantically and try to run away, but Jess is there already shoving me toward the stage. Everything becomes a blur. Within seconds, I find myself standing on the stage staring at the curious crowd. For a moment, I stop breathing. I can't do this. Other than Jess and my brothers, and my singing lessons years ago, no one has heard me sing. Now, I'm about to do that in front of a sea of familiar and unfamiliar faces.

It's a baptism by fire. My heart is beating fast as a hummingbird's wings.

How did this happen?

I'm so going to screw this up.

Tyler passes the microphone to me and meets my gaze with a questioning look, and I know he senses my fear, my hesitation. With the slightest smile, he reaches for my hand, leans in to me, and whispers in my ear, "What song would you like to sing?"

"I don't know," I stammer, fear clogging my throat. "Sorry, reflex."

"It'll be fine. You have a beautiful voice."

"That was at the store, and I was alone."

"I'll be here." He takes my hand. "Do you know 'Dust to Dust' by the Civil Wars?"

I nod. "You want to sing a duet?"

"Yes, I'd love to sing with you," he says, and I believe him. His eyes speak the truth.

He tells his band what song we'll be singing and stands by his microphone. I'm not too far away from him, but if I stretch my hand, I can't touch him. After a three-beat count from the drummer, the lead guitarist starts playing a few chords, and then the bass guitarist and the drummer join as well, giving a soulful, solemn vibe which makes all my fears go away. I wait for the four-beat count before putting the microphone close to my mouth.

Nerves sizzle like wires. Shit, I'm about to do something big.

I inhale a deep shaky breath and check in with myself, finding my bravery, to go forward. Often...well...always...I live at the intersection of needing adventure and feeling shy. Typically, I give the shy aspect of my personality free rein, now it's time for the adventurous aspect to have its chance on stage.

I glance over at Jess. She gives me a thumbs-up and a wide smile, and I nod at Tyler, silently letting him know I'm ready. He takes the lead, and I fall in with him effortlessly. Closing my eyes, I allow myself to feel the song and let the lyrics have meaning to me in this moment, like I'm talking to someone in the audience. The song is an anthem for the lonely. Sometimes, we come across somebody who thinks they're hiding their pain, but if we're all honest, nobody is very good at it.

A surge of energy shoots through me. I sing the last line of the first verse and then open my eyes and look at Tyler.

The subtle rise of his eyebrow indicates his surprise. Up until now he didn't know I could sing. He doesn't know singing is my therapy, the place I go to for healing. My catharsis. He doesn't know I've dreamed of this moment and that all I want is to be a singer.

I start the first line of the second verse, and Tyler sings along. When I start the chorus, Tyler joins in, his voice a lower octave. The music becomes my external heartbeat, and the lyrics are sweet vibrations in my soul. Warmth spreads through my chest. I can sing these poetic words forever—words about two people who have been lonely for too long, breaking down the walls they've both built up as they fall in love.

Tyler and I exchange momentary glances; each time our eyes meet, we smile. He's like a mirror reflecting me, both of us longing for something more.

We move to the third verse, harmonizing like we've always performed together. We sing in a near-whisper, backed by a tiptoeing combination of guitar and drums. Tyler moves closer to me, and we belt out the chorus together, feeling every word.

Sparks fly in every direction. We're having a conversation on stage, making every inflection count.

When we end, our eyes stay connected, both of us breathing heavily in our own little world until the crowd's cheers cut through the silent moment, and the bubble pops.

Jess waits for me on the side of the stage, and I rush into her arms.

"You were so good."

The band joins us, and we all spend a moment on introductions before Tyler pulls me away. "Let me take you out for real this time. Give me your number?"

I shake my head. "I don't know if that's a good idea."

He tugs my phone from my hand and grins. Ten missed calls from Rueben. I groan and snatch it back.

Then he offers me his phone. "Please. I want to see you again."

There's sincerity in his tone, but also something else, apprehension maybe? It's that little kernel of doubt that helps me decide. I quickly punch in my full name—Millie Cantal—my number and save the contact info.

Jess bounds to my side excitedly showing me the autographs she got from everyone. I stare down at the eleventh missed call from my brother. "It's time to go. Let me get you home."

5

TYLER

The light in Millie's green eyes as she stared at me across a microphone is the first thing I think about when I wake up the next day, and immediately, all I can think about is hearing her voice again. Maybe another man would try to play it cool, but I call her later in the afternoon.

Her phone rings and I chant, "Please answer. Please answer. Please answer."

When I pulled her on the stage last night, her hand trembled in mine, but when we finished, she seemed happy, content in a way I haven't seen from her yet. To be fair, I don't know her well, but damn, I want to.

After the fifth ring, my heart clogging my throat, she picks up with a tentative hello.

"Millie? It's Tyler." Smooth. Way to charm the lady.

She clears her throat gently, and after a long pause she whispers, "Hi."

"Are you at work today?"

There's a shuffle and then her answer. "Yes, but I'm on a break. You have good timing, actually."

I try to picture her face in my mind. Her vivid green eyes staring up at me, the scent of her when we stood so close together last night had been both arousing and comforting.

"Oh, well, I wanted to ask if I can take you to dinner. I'll be that guy and simply say, I've been thinking about you today."

"I've been thinking about you, too. I had so much fun singing with you last night."

My heart gives a funny little jolt at her response and the warmth in her tone. I'm glad she's not angry at me for shoving her into the spotlight.

"So then, dinner? There's a great place near me I'd love to take you."

There's a long pause, and I clutch my phone tighter, praying she'll say yes, let me spend a few more minutes with her.

A refrain hits me as I wait, and I quickly dig out the small spiral notebook in my pocket and scribble it down.

"I don't think I can, honestly. I'm always working. My brother and I own the store, and we juggle most of the schedule between us."

I'm about to cut in, make my case, but she continues. "We have a couple other employees, but they're mostly seasonal, and one of them is flaky. It's like pulling teeth to get him to show up to his shifts. I often have to cover."

I falter, searching my brain for other options. I'd drive to her house and sit outside with her if it's the only way I can see her. This is insane. I barely know Millie. For whatever reason I can't get her out of my mind.

Damn. I can't remember the last time a woman has affected me this much. Actually, never. That's the answer.

I hopefully strip the disappointment from my tone. "We

could meet before your shift for breakfast, or afterward, grab a late appetizer? Anything, really. I simply want to spend a little more time with you."

The soft chuckle from her loosens the knot she's tied around my chest. "You're very persistent."

"I know what I want," I say. "I'll take you to dinner, lunch, breakfast, a snack, anything you'll give me. Dinner is only my first choice."

"Okay, okay. I'll go with you."

I spin around in the tight confines of my kitchen and silently send up a thank you to the universe. "Great. I'll pick yo—"

"I'll meet you."

The force in her previously whispered tone gives me pause. "Are you sure? It's no problem."

"Totally sure. I don't mind meeting you."

"How about Holidaze Arcade in Kissme Bay?" I suggest the old school arcade. There is a bar in the back. Pacman and old arcade games. Perfect for dates, I guess.

"Sure. Friday works best. The store is usually slow, and I can get away after we close."

I nod and then remember she can't see me, so I roll my eyes at myself. "Okay, see you on Friday. It was nice talking to you again."

We hang up, and I can't keep the grin from my face as I climb into my car and drive to see my Gramps. No doubt, he'll take one look at me and know I've met someone, but I can't bring myself to care. Not when I get to spend more time with Millie soon.

When I pull up to the familiar white house, I take a moment to let the present and the memories to line up. I can still remember how it felt to have my Gramps lead me up those well-maintained steps to the front door. And how I skinned my knees playing on that sidewalk out front so many times.

Before my parents died, I only saw Gramps sporadically. But, afterward, he was all I had. He did his best for me. Something he's never stopped doing. He couldn't have known what that meant. I try to remind him now, as an adult, how much he means to me.

Despite a wave of melancholy threatens to choke me, I push it aside, focusing on the good things: Gramps, Millie saying yes to our date.

I find Gramps settled into his favorite chair, a TV tray set up in front of him, an episode of the Deadliest Catch queued up and ready on the screen. Another tray is set up in front of the couch, and I settle in to spend some time with him.

He heaves himself out of the chair, and I hop up to help, but he waves me back down.

"I'm just getting a beer. You want one?"

I shove a bite of flaky fish in my mouth—it's delicious, as always—and swallow. "No, Gramps, you know I don't drink."

The sound of beer bottles, crashing together as my face is slammed into a table, hits me hard.

A memory. Only a memory.

I push away the plate, knowing Gramps will protest, but I can't eat when the past swamps me. Most of the time, I let them pass through, fade to nothing, but occasionally, they linger, and my parents' misdeeds haunt me.

He returns with a beer for himself and a bottle of water for me. I crack the top and guzzle half.

"You should think about coming with me. It's the

anniversary, and I hoped you would this time," Gramps presses, over the sounds of the men shouting to each other on the TV fishing boat.

I don't answer, even though I know he'll keep asking, and tug my plate back to the edge of the tray. Gramps is a marvel in the kitchen with a fish. Most of them he catches himself, but often his best friend Greg, who lives next door, brings some food over to help when Gramps' arthritis acts up.

"So what's new with you, Gramps? Planning a trip to the lake this weekend?"

It's amazing how quickly and excitedly the old man talks about his hobby. I enjoy listening to him. Each little anecdote he shares gives me a glimpse of the kind man who raised me. And all over again, I try to see how my mother came from this man. She was sweet enough when sober, but once the beer, and later, liquor, came into the picture, she became an entirely different person.

I shove away the memories again and focus as Gramps explains a new lure he just bought, and how he and Greg are going to take Greg's small boat to a large lake up north on the upcoming weekend.

"What about that nice woman you met at the community center?" I prompt, waiting for his reaction.

As usual, he sputters, tearing his focus from the TV. "Well, she's very nice. I have a standing date for dominoes at the senior center. We play every other Sunday."

"Dominoes, huh? Is that what the kids are calling it these days?"

He narrows his eyes and points his fork at me. "Eat your food, boy, before I comment on the state of your love life."

And all over again Millie consumes my thoughts. I want

to tell him about her, but not yet. I want to keep her to myself for a little while longer.

I finish eating long before Gramps does and sit back to watch him enjoy his show. Thankfully, he doesn't bring up the anniversary of my parents' accident again, or the ensuing trip he plans to take to their graves. I respect him more than anyone, but I don't owe them a damn thing.

We sit in companionable silence, watching his show, and every so often, he'll interject with a comment on the boat, or the fishermen. It's easy to spend time with him, and I feel guilty for letting the memories of my parents taint the time he and I get to share.

Especially, since I'll see him less when I make it to Nashville. It's been a dream of mine for years to head out there, make a name for myself in the songwriting world. Would Gramps come with me? I could set him up in a little house, show him the best fishing spots.

No. The idea fizzles. Gramps will never leave this place. The house he raised my mother in. The house his wife died in. The house he saved me in. I couldn't ask it of him, anyway.

After dinner is finished, and I wash the dishes and leave them to dry on a tidy rack on the counter, Gramps waits by the door to usher me out.

I give him a hug which he half returns. Never a man for sentimental displays of affection. But the love is there in his eyes when he pats my cheek gently. I'm taller than him now, which I always find strange, no matter how old I get.

As I walk out, I remind him. "Don't forget to send me pictures of your biggest catches. I want to see."

"Oh, I don't want to be a bother," he says in that smoky baritone.

I quickly demonstrate how to text an image for the tenth time then walk to my car.

By the time I reach home, he's sent me a picture of the last catch he made, and I smile all the way to my loft door.

6

MILLIE

Nothing beats French toast in the morning. A text hits my phone as I climb out of the shower, and I smile as David sends me a dopey smiley face and a picture of an enormous stack of French toast, butter and syrup streaming over the sides.

My mouth waters, and no doubt, he knows I'll show up.

When I make it to the diner, Rueben is already parked in his favorite booth in the back corner. The red vinyl worn from decades of use. The tables scrubbed raw but always clean. Even the worn floors are spotless under dusty boots. The Diner is what everyone in town calls the place, even though the sign on the outside reads Virgin Street Diner.

I slide into the booth, and Rueben eyes me over the edge of his newspaper. He's still angry about me going out with Tyler, but I tell myself I don't care. When he and David learn to treat me like an adult, I might consider his opinions more. Until then, neither of them get any say about my personal life.

Even as I lie to myself, I feel guilty about how I spoke to Rueben. But I let the silence stand and wait for David to bring breakfast. The server doesn't even bother to come to our table, since David will take a break and join us.

When the food is passed around, I groan as the scent of melted butter and cinnamon reaches me. The bacon follows, and I dive into the food. Breakfast has to be my favorite meal of the day. Especially, when my brother cooks.

I glance up at them, mouth stuffed full, but they aren't eating.

It takes me a minute to swallow. "What is it? You both look like someone's died."

Rueben maintains eye contact with me; David looks a little more uncomfortable. He's sitting backward on a chair he dragged to the end of the booth. Both of my brothers are big hulking men, and it's comical to see them try to sit in a booth side by side.

David tugs off his beanie and fluffs his hair, the same shade of dark brown as mine. Now I know something is up.

"What's the problem? You're both scaring me." I jerk the bacon plate toward me on the table and riffle through the pieces until I find some extra crispy ones.

Rueben clears his throat and leans forward, all business. "We don't want you seeing that guy anymore."

My eyes widen as surprise courses through me. "What?"

I search his gaze and take stock of every detail. He's not kidding. Unable to believe what's happening, I glance at David, who's now adopted Rueben's resolve and is staring me down as well.

Rueben continues. "We don't want you seeing him anymore, and that's final."

This can't be happening. They're talking to me as if I'm a child. Frustrated, I toss the bacon onto the plate with more force than strictly necessary. "Are you joking right now? Last I checked, I'm an adult." I huff out a breath. "I can decide for myself who I go out with or not. And not that it's any of your business, but I went out with Jess, not with Tyler. He was playing in the band, and we only spent a moment together, not that I have to explain myself to either of you."

David cuts in. "Will you please trust us to know what's best for you, like we've always done?"

Perfect. A subtle reminder that they were the ones who took care of me when our Mom and Dad died. Way to pack on the guilt.

I glare at my oldest brother and then shift my focus back to Rueben. The obvious ringleader of this escapade. "Thanks so much for dragging my business out to be weighed and judged by both of you. I don't appreciate being talked about behind my back, nor do I think it's acceptable for you to treat me like a child when I'm almost 25."

Of course, Rueben won't let it go. "Everyone in town is talking about you two singing together. They are saying all sorts of things, Millie."

Awesome. So, it's not just my brothers, now it's the entire town. "The town can take a hike, along with both of you. I'm not a little girl anymore."

Rueben slams his hand on the table, setting the dishes rattling. "Then stop acting like one. We're only trying to do what's best for you. Don't make this worse than it already is. What were you thinking getting on stage with him?"

"I was thinking that he's a nice man and wanted to sing with me. And you know what? I enjoyed it. What's wrong with that? You both know how much I love to sing." I huff out a frustrated breath. "Jesus, you guys worked extra hours to pay for my voice and piano lessons. Why would you not want me to enjoy my passion?"

David huffs from beside me. "Come on, Millie, you can't

still be dreaming of becoming a singer? You've always had a nice voice, but it's not a realistic career goal."

I shift my gaze to him, letting him see how much his comment hurt me. "And what is a realistic career goal? A line cook at a diner? Or a hardware store cashier? Since you're making suggestions and all, is that how you'd prefer I spend my life?"

I left them at the table sputtering. Not even French toast can calm me down right now. If I were a stronger woman I would have gone home, but instead, I head to work as usual. When Rueben shows up, he better steer clear.

Except, as the day goes on, Rueben doesn't come to the hardware store, leaving me stuck to man the counter all day, forcing me to miss my date with Tyler.

I'm seething as I text Tyler apologizing. He doesn't seem angry, at least from what I can tell via text. After some back and forth, I ask him to meet me at the pub down the street. With the local night spot being so close to work, I'll have enough time to change and get ready before I see him.

He's already there when I arrive, and I sweep my hair around my neck, pulling it forward, sudden and swift butterflies erupting in my belly.

I walk over, and when I get within inches of him he gives me a devastating smile. I can't help but smile back.

"Do you want something to drink? Eat?"

I force out a long sigh, calming myself down. It's just a date. "Yes please, white wine."

He nods and heads off toward the bar.

When he returns, he's clutching a bottled water and passes me a glass of wine. I eye his glass, and he gently says, "I don't drink."

"Oh, Okay."

He gestures at the empty high top he parked us at. "Do you want to play pool?"

Oh, no. Can you scare a man away by being bad at a bar game? "Um...I don't know. I'm not really great at pool."

His smile disarms me all over again. I hide my blush with the wineglass then set it aside.

He places his water beside my wine. "Has anyone ever taught you how to play? Can I show you?"

I nod. "Sure."

The sticks are on the wall, and he grabs one, then hands it to me. "Ready?"

When I step up to the table, my hands shake as he comes behind me, not pressing into me but wrapping himself around me. His long, powerful arms around mine, he gently leans me over the edge of the table and points down the end of the stick. I can feel the heat of him, the strength, and it arouses me, making me shiver.

"Make sure you line up the stick with the white ball." His voice is low, and a little husky. His breath is warm against my skin, shooting tingles through me. I can only nod around the lump in my throat. "The first strike is about power. Send the balls spinning out hard, and then you can see where everything falls."

Gently, he shows me how to hold the cue stick, he calls it, and then lets me follow through with the hit.

The balls break apart with a loud crack, but I'm not even looking. My focus is on the heavy weight of his hand against my lower back.

"Well done. Look, you sunk two of the solids. So, that's going to be your color."

We play through the game, and I suspect he lets me win. But every time I line up a shot, he comes around to monitor the way I line up the stick. Each touch is another spark adding to the fire already raging in my belly.

When we finish, he gently steers me toward the high top again. "I want to know about you. How did you and your brother end up owning a hardware store together?"

I cup my wine for support and settle onto the bar stool. The way his gray shirt clings to his broad shoulders is distracting, but I drag my focus back to his question. "Well, it belonged to my parents. But they died when I was young, leaving it to my brothers and me. David, my other brother, didn't want it, he's more of a free spirit. So, Rueben took it over, and when I was old enough, I started helping out, too. They raised me after my parents' death."

"My parents are gone as well. My grandfather raised me. How did your parents die?"

My memories of the accident are vague and frankly I'd rather not talk about it on our date, but still I answer, "a car accident off Route 220."

His brow furrows, a shadow of sadness in his eyes as he takes a sip of his bottled water. Then, as if he shook himself back to reality, he says, "I'm so sorry to hear about your loss. How about a lighter topic then? What do you like to do for fun?"

A part of me is tempted to ask more. What happened to his parents? How come he's not having a beer like almost everyone in the room. But then I decide he's right, it's not really talk for a bar...or a first date conversation.

"Well, it's not too far off the original question," I answer. "I love to hike. My parents were big hikers, and being out in nature makes me feel close to them."

He asks about my mom, and I enjoy talking about her. I can't remember much, but I remember her eyes (same as mine) and her perfume. When he listens, it's as if he is locking on to every word and filing it away. He makes me feel heard unlike anyone has before.

After I finish my wine, I check my phone, and notice a few missed calls from my brothers. "I should really go."

He nods. "Let me walk you to your car."

Butterflies flap their wings crazy low in my belly. I wonder if he'll kiss me. Just the thought makes my nipples contract with greedy anticipation. When we get to my car, I fiddle with the keys, not brave enough to do anything but smile.

"I guess this is goodnight," he says.

A flashing sign from across the street bathes his face in alternating green and blue, and it's a mesmerizing sight. If there was ever a moment I wish I could take a picture of and save forever, it's this one.

But I won't be pulling out my phone and snapping a creepy pic of his face, so instead I say, "Um, yes."

He lifts a hand, and fingers the end of my hair then moves in so close I can feel his lean, powerful body pressed up against me. Tension—the good kind—sparks in the air. Goosebumps bloom along my skin. The slow burn of desire crackles.

"Millie..." his voice trails as if he's asking for my permission to kiss me.

"Yes," I answer in a whisper, granting him the invitation he sought.

A silence falls between us for the first time, not the bad kind. It's comfortable and we linger in it for a second like two people who aren't ready to say goodbye, two people who crave something more.

His face drifts slightly closer to me, his masculine scent floods my nose. The possibility of a kiss hangs in the air. My breath hitches from him being so near.

He cups the back of my neck with his hand. "I had a great time with you tonight."

Desire burns through me. My mind latches on to the possibility of kissing Tyler and already I'm picturing our lips together. *Please kiss me.*

After the longest minute, he leans in and kisses my cheek. The spicy scent of him wraps around me, and the soft warm weight of his lips lights me up further.

When he leans back I can only murmur, "thank you."

He takes a couple steps back, still watching me. I climb into my car, dropping into my seat, I give him a wave and turn over the ignition.

Except nothing happens.

Mindful he's still standing there, I switch the ignition again. It makes a grinding sound.

What the heck? My old car may have finally reached its limit.

Frustrated, I blow out a breath and look up. Tyler is watching me, a concerned look on his face, then he knocks on the window. I roll it down by the handle. "Sorry, it won't start."

"We can get it towed, but you still need a ride home." His gorgeous brown eyes lock with mine, a question in his gaze. "Let me take you home, then."

7

———

TYLER

Taking her home is such a bad idea. Especially with my brain reeling from everything I learned about her parents. But I can't resist a few more minutes with her. Because of that I tell myself the death of her parents occurring at the same place my parents crashed into another car while they were drunk driving is merely coincidental.

She waves at the sidewalk in front of the pub. "I can just walk. I'm right down the road."

I shake my head. "My Gramps and your brothers would murder me if I let you walk home on your own. I'll see you to your door."

When she ducks her chin and gives me a little nod, I know I've got her. She starts toward the sidewalk, and I follow, matching her pace.

"Do you have any shows coming up?" she asks, as we walk.

I'm tempted to tug her hand into mine and interlace our fingers. After showing her how to play pool, I want to touch her, more of her, all of her. But I also don't want to scare her away. So, I shove my hands into my pockets and keep walking. "Actually, yes. I'll be on the road with the band next week. We're headed north for a few days, so I'll be gone."

We walk in silence for a moment until we're standing outside a door which leads up to a little apartment above a storefront. She dangles her keys between her fingers, a pink wash staining her cheeks. "Do you want to come up for a second?"

I'm not naïve enough to think she's inviting me up for sex. Not with that blush. But I smile and nod. "I should really make sure you get to your door."

She leads me up the stairs, unlocks the door, and gestures for me to enter.

I look around as I step over the threshold. It's a small apartment, but clean, orderly, decorated in earth tones and soft creams.

"It's nice. I'm sure as hell not taking you to my place until I clean it up some. I'm gone so much, it gets a little crazy—especially, when we're in peak tour season."

She shuts the door and drops her things on a table by the entrance. I study her and ball my hands in my pockets. She's watching me just as closely as I am her, her eyes glinting with lust and desire.

It's worse now, since I know what her soft curves feel like against me. I can't resist, so I step forward, closing some distance. "Do you have to work tomorrow?"

She nods. "I always have to work."

I gently drag a few strands of hair from her face and tuck them behind ear. "I haven't stopped thinking about you. Not since the moment I first saw you, not since I heard you sing. I shouldn't... I know I should—"

She steps forward, grabs the back of my neck, and mashes her lips with mine. I let her lead, control the kiss, give and take what she wants, what she needs.

But then her tongue sweeps over my lips, and I lose my fight with my control. My head spins. My heart beats a fast tempo. I seize her face between my hands and carefully walk her backward to the wall. When her back hits with a little thump, I take over. Achingly slow, I trace the seam of her lips with my tongue, and when she opens to me, I delve between her lips. She clutches at my waist, her hands gripping my t-shirt in her fists.

It's her little moan that undoes me completely. Everything in my being doesn't want this moment to end. I reach down and haul her up, her legs wrap around my hips, and I hold tight to her back and thigh as I devour every inch of her mouth. There's not a single bit I don't explore with my teeth, my tongue, or my lips.

She arches her hips into me, and reality crashes around us hard. I blink and pull away. Her eyes are heavy-lidded and hazy as she stares down at me. Her lips are swollen and pink from my own. My cock is hard as steel in my jeans. It would only take a few steps to lay her on the couch and take her right here. From the look on her face, I don't think she'd say no.

"Are you okay?" she asks, as I stand there staring at her.

I let her slide down my body and hiss as she grazes my length through my pants. "Yeah, fine. I'm sorry. I didn't mean to..."

She shakes her head. "No, I kissed you."

I finally step away from her, the cold air settling between us. "I should go."

When she nods, I know I've made the right choice. She's not ready for this, and to be honest, neither am I. There's too much at stake. My gut keeps telling me Millie and I are connected. It's time I find out if our pasts have crossed paths long before we ever met.

She holds the door open for me, and I walk out. Her wave is the last thing I see as she shuts the heavy white wooden door then locks it with a loud clunk.

I press my hand to the door for just a second, savoring the last lingering moments of her body clinging to mine.

Then I head back to my car. I have a question blazing in my brain I haven't been able to ignore since we left the bar. It's a question that will keep me from sleeping until I have a straight answer.

It's late when I make it to Gramps' house. I let myself in with the key and find him asleep in his chair in front of the TV. When he can't sleep, he ends up watching TV until he finally drifts off. I hate it but haven't been successful in talking him out of it.

I gently shake his shoulder. "Gramps. Wake up, please. I need to talk to you."

He opens his eyes and blinks at me. "Tyler, what are you doing here so late?"

I crouch beside his chair, so he doesn't have to strain his neck to meet my eyes.

"Tell me everything about the night my parents died. Someone else died."

He doesn't ask questions or feign ignorance. I've always loved that about him. "Two," Gramps says.

Something kicks in my gut hard. I drop my face into my hands and shake my head, then I lose my balance and settle back onto my ass on the floor. "Why didn't you tell me?"

"Every time I bring up your parents, you suddenly have somewhere else to be, or something else to do. And when it happened, you were too young to deal with that knowledge."

Despair rises from my stomach and blocks my throat.

"They left behind three children. Two boys and a girl named Millie."

He furrows his brow and shrugs. "Well, I don't know their names. They live in Cherry Falls. The accident was on Route 220, right by the Cherry Falls exit."

I can barely breathe around this new truth. It doesn't even feel like a truth, more like a lie that had been waiting to ambush me at the right moment.

Guilt stabs at me. What my parents had done I could not un-do. Innocent lives were cut short. Three children were robbed of their parents, and Millie's brothers were forced to play the adults.

Remorse hits me like a sledgehammer. How, of all the women I meet in the world, would she be the one who draws me in so much? And now, I won't be able to look at her without her seeing the truth.

As much as it hurts, I have to push her away. The shows I have over the next week will help. I'll tell her my schedule is busy, and we can't see each other. And then, I'll be a coward and never show my face where she might be present.

"Why all these questions?" Gramps asks.

I sigh and drag myself up onto the couch. "There's this girl... I met a girl...her name is Millie Cantal."

"Shit," he breathes.

"My parents killed hers that night."

8

———

TYLER

The shows blur together, a hazy mess of songs, music, bars, and crowds. I can't focus, and I know the band is worrying about me, wondering if I'm going to snap out of it.

How do I come back from this? What in the world could possibly make things right for what Millie lost? I know the answer, even though I ask myself the same questions over and over again.

Nothing.

My parents...ruining my life even from the grave. It's a special kind of skill.

Gramps calls twice while we're out of town, and while I answer his calls, I have nothing to say. It's not his fault, but I feel like this bomb should have been dropped a lot sooner. Not that I'm blaming my grandfather. To be fair, every time he brought up my parents, I always refused to engage, and I take full responsibility on that front.

The band drags me on stage again, and I try to summon the joy, the enthusiasm, anything to put on the show these people expect, that they paid for. It's hard, but I manage, barely.

When a love song queues up, my mind immediately goes to Millie. How she felt in my arms, how she tasted on my lips. Each of the little whimpers she made.

I sing the song to her, for her, knowing she'll never look at me from a crowd again. The words lose their meaning as I pour myself into them, giving myself to Millie, and the crowd in a way I haven't in a long time. Not since I learned the detachment needed for the job.

When the last strains fade away, the patrons erupt in screaming applause. I'm dragged into a bow and waved off the stage.

Immediately, we're swarmed by women waiting their turn to meet us. Hands are grabbing me, touching me, from my neck to stomach. I hate this part, even more so now that not a single one of them is Millie.

Cash and Gavin are eating up the attention. Coby stands to the side, surveying the scene with disgust. One look at my face, and she grabs my arm and hauls me back to the dressing rooms.

She closes the door behind us and waves her arms. "What the hell is wrong with you, man? You've been off since we started this tour."

I flop on the worn leather couch and scrub my hands over my head. "I know. I'm sorry."

She sits on a mirrored counter. "I figured. Cash and Gavin don't buy your little 'I'm tired' spiel either. But this whole thing tonight—those women mob you guys, and you look like you're ready to start throwing punches. Tell me what's wrong."

As much as I want to confide in someone, I don't want the band having to deal with my crap any more than they already do. "It's complicated."

"And when isn't it? I'm a big girl. I can keep up."

I double over and brace my hands on my knees. The band knows my history. They know my life before Gramps took me in, and we've been friends since high school. This is just another page in my story to them. But, confessing it feels like another weakness added to my list.

"The night my parents died, two other people died. They were Millie's parents." I can't look at her as she processes.

"Fuck."

Yeah. Pretty much. "I didn't know. Gramps didn't tell me at the time because he thought I was too young to know. I found out when she and I were talking about it."

"Oh, shit, does she know?"

I drag a hand through my hair. "No, she has no idea. I fucking like this girl, Coby."

The mirror behind her squeaks as she leans into it. "What are you going to do?"

The familiar guilt stabs at me, tearing off little chunks of my soul. It takes all my resolve to say the next words. "Stay away from her."

She snorts. "Good luck with that. I saw the way you two looked at each other."

9

———

MILLIE

Work sucks. The day sucks. Everything sucks. Usually, I try to stay optimistic, even when customers are difficult or my car craps out. But today, on the fifth day since I last heard from Tyler, I just want to throw things.

He said he'd be out of town on tour. I assumed it meant he'd at least call me. Let me know he enjoyed our date or the kiss we shared afterward.

But nothing. Not a damn thing.

I throw the duster on the counter, and it flops off the edge onto the floor. "UGGG!" I shout at the fluffy yellow tool.

When I explained my frustration to Jess, she told me to just text him. Every night since we kissed, I've opened my text app and stared at it, hoping to see something different from the confirmation of our last date. Except nothing ever comes. I can't text him because I don't know what to say. *Sorry I'm such a terrible kisser you decided not to contact me afterward?*

But it didn't feel like he hated it. The way he'd picked me

up and pressed into me against the wall, I thought I felt... something. He even moaned into my lips, a sound that haunts me. I hate feeling this way. I hate that another person can have so much power over me. Someone that I barely know.

Ha. Joke's on me.

I go around the counter and snag the duster off the floor. Rueben wanders in from the warehouse. "Hey, you okay? Still mad at us?"

"If you have a comment on my personal life, then yes. If not, then no. Did you need something?"

David walks in the front door joining us. My guard immediately goes up. This is feeling like an ambush. I watch him, ready to take them both on.

David sits a Styrofoam container on the counter, spins it toward me, and opens it with a flourish. French toast, melty and delicious, greets me from the wide interior.

"Peace offering," David says, holding out a plastic fork for me to take.

Still not trusting them, I accept the utensil and stare between them. "What's going on?"

Rueben snags a piece of bacon from the container and I glare. "We noticed you seem kind of down lately. Just wanted to cheer you up."

"This helps." I shove a bite into my mouth and moan around the cinnamon flavor.

David leans on the counter. "You know mom loved French toast. She made it every Sunday. But it was a whole big thing. Whipped cream, sprinkles, chocolate sauce, cereal bits. I think that's why you love it so much."

I swallow the sudden clog in my throat. "She did? I had no idea. I mean, I can't remember that."

Rueben interjects. "I'll see if I can find some pictures."

"I'd like that." I whisper.

David nods and waves at us, and Rueben heads back to the warehouse, leaving me alone with my spoils.

I decide to focus on good things instead of wallowing. Perhaps it's a good thing Tyler ghosted. He's charming, good looking. I could have fallen for him hard. And then what? A heartbreak. Maybe he'd end up cheating on me the same way David's wife cheated on him.

Yeah, no thanks.

I tuck an earbud in my ear and turn on one of my favorite country songs. The familiar music soothes me, and I take another bite of my French toast. Ahh, food makes everything better.

I dust the shelves that line the main retail area, careful to move the products so I can get into the back of the shelves.

As the chorus blasts in my ear, I sing along, getting into the rhythm, already feeling like myself again.

I'm really getting into the song, dancing and singing. The bell over the door rings and I finish the song before popping my head out from between the shelves. "Can I help..."

I expect someone hunting for paint, or nails, or a new wrench. Instead, Tyler stands just inside the door, a bouquet of daisies in his hand.

The next song plays, and I fumble my phone from my pocket to shut it off. When I look up again, Tyler has advanced into the store. Sunlight gleams off his sharp cheekbones, shooting flecks through his brown eyes.

My heart leaps with joy at seeing him. Stupid. Stupid heart.

Play it cool.

I clear my throat. "So, you *are* alive? I wasn't sure." My

tone is biting, and I hate that he can detect that his behavior has hurt me.

"I stopped at the flower patch." He holds out the flowers, a tentative smile spreading his lips.

"Is that it? You don't have an excuse or anything? You're just sorry?" I huff and sit my phone and earbuds on the counter. "I knew you were going out of town, but I thought you'd at least send a text. You just disappeared."

"You've been on my mind every second, every minute, every hour."

I cross my arms over my chest, well aware that my vibe screams I'm pissed off and I don't care. "Was it because I kissed you?"

"I thought staying away was the right thing to do. At least that's what I tried to do."

"What does that mean?"

"Nothing. The truth is, I missed you."

Our gazes lock, my frazzled nerves jumping all together, and in different directions.

"As for our kiss..." He crosses the space, puts the flowers near my phone. In a second, his arms are around me, and his lips are on mine. He tastes the same, smells the same, feels the same.

A part of me wants to hold on to the anger, but eventually the pull I feel toward him takes over. I part my lips and thread my fingers through his hair as he kisses me slow and deep. We continue like this, lips melding, tongues sliding, our bodies arching into each other in a slow rhythm until he slowly breaks the connection. I blink back to reality and know my face must be burning.

"It definitely wasn't the kiss." He sweeps back my hair, and his lips crack into a smile. "But I'm sorry. You deserve better. I want to get to know you. Take you out. See you smile. Will you let me do that?"

He seems sincere, and I nod, not really wanting to hold a grudge about it. I push aside any doubts and say, "Okay then."

Rueben chooses the perfect time to saunter back in. "What are you doing here?"

I groan and swat at his arm when he gets close enough. "Be nice."

Of course he ignores me, making forceful eye contact with Tyler. They are similar in height, even if my brother has about thirty pounds on him.

"I asked what you're doing here?"

Tyler extends his hand. "Hi, I'm Tyler Yates. I'm here to see Millie."

Rueben narrows his eyes and doesn't shake the offered hand. "I know who you are. While I can't seem to talk my sister out of seeing you, know that I'm watching you."

"Oh my God," I whisper, completely mortified. "Rueben, go to the back. You're being ridiculous."

Rueben eyes the flowers on the counter, turns his back, and leaves. I have zero doubt he's in listening distance, though.

"I'm so sorry about that. My brothers are both really protective of me."

Tyler tugs my hands into his. "Please, let me take you to lunch. I've been thinking about you every day since I left."

"Sure, give me a minute." I stick my head into the warehouse and yell "back in one hour" to my brother. A grunt from Rueben indicates he heard me, but it's Jacob Sten, one of the guys who usually works in the warehouse who strolls in. "Thanks, Jacob."

He nods at Tyler in silent acknowledgement then turns to me. "Be careful."

"Always." I grab my purse and smile at Tyler. "Let's go."

We step onto the sidewalk. I'm not super hungry since I had a mid-morning French toast binge.

"Where do you want to go? There's a diner up the road."

"Virgin Street Diner."

"Yeah. I hear awesome things about it. Everyone loves it."

I snort. No way on earth am I going on a date with Tyler where my brother works. "Nope, not there. How about coffee and a snack at Bela's bakery? I'm not super hungry yet. But I do want to spend time with you and hear about the tour."

When he takes my hand and interlaces our fingers, he gives me almost a look of defiance. As if he's waiting for the powers that be to rip our hands apart. I smile and squeeze his fingers.

He leads me down the sidewalk to the bistro, and we quickly claim a table in the corner. The coffee is hot, and he asks me how I take it (three sugars, two creams) and repeats it as if he's trying to memorize it.

My heart gives a jolt at the thought of him sticking around long enough to know my coffee order.

I settle in with my mug and watch as he tears into a chocolate filled croissant, his lips closing around the pastry in one giant bite. I swear watching him is like watching the Duke in Bridgerton licking that spoon. I gulp, every part of me quivers.

He stops eating and stares. I shake myself, sure my face is bright pink. "So how was the tour? Did you have fun with the band? Meet any interesting people?"

When he drags his eyes from mine and doesn't answer, I'm not sure if I should push, or leave it alone.

"We had a good time. I'm enjoying the shows, but sometimes, I just want to be in a studio with my notebook and a pen, writing the music."

I take a sip of my coffee. "You don't want to be famous?"

He shrugs. "Not necessarily. I want to be successful, but at the things about music I can't live without. Songwriting is my passion, not performing."

The way he sang the other night, I wouldn't have guessed. He's a natural on stage; people can't take their eyes off him.

"What about you?" he prompts.

"Me?" I squeak.

"You love to sing. I can see it so clearly. I saw it the other night, and I can hear it in your voice when you sing along to your music while you clean. Why aren't you out there trying to make it?"

"It's a long story."

He leans back in his seat. "We got all day. Tell me, Millie, what's holding you back?"

"Nothing's holding me back."

He studies my face for a beat and I shift under the scrutiny.

"It's not that I think my brothers are just keeping me here," I say staring down at my coffee for a second before meeting his gaze. "I guess I sort of feel like I owe them for raising me when they didn't have to."

He furrows his brow and leans in. "I'm sure they wouldn't say you owe them."

"They're a bit protective." I shrug. "I'm sure my parents' death didn't help."

"I'm sorry about what happened to them."

"It's okay. I just wish I could talk to the driver you know... and tell them how careless it was to drive drunk. Innocent people died. Heck..." I shake my head. "They died too. I wonder if they had children."

Tyler opens his mouth as if he's about to say something then closes it. We sit in companionable silence, broken only when Tyler lets out a deep breath, and says, "I have a proposition."

His words pique my curiosity. I lift a brow. "Oh."

"My band is going out again." A smile widens over his handsome face. "We'll be on the road for two days. Come with us."

My heart kicks then stops. Excitement courses through my veins. I'd love to travel with him and see places outside of Cherry Falls. I've dreamed of this. But even if I can leave town for a few days, Tyler is in a band. "I'd just be in the way."

"Nonsense."

"Tyler..."

"Millie, I'm really sorry about not contacting you the last few days. If that's what's stopping you from saying yes..."

"Well, there's that too."

"I'm not sure what's happening but I can't stay away from you." He pulls my second hand from the coffee mug to hold it. "I want you there with me. I want you to see what it's like. Feel the energy. I think you'd love it more than anything."

I should say no. I should just say no. Except, when I open my mouth, the only thing that comes out is: "Yes."

10

TYLER

Yesterday before Millie returned to the shop I convinced her to let me take her for a hike. She sounded so fond of the activity when she confessed her love for it at the bar. And all I can think about is making her happy, since obviously she was upset with my lack of contact.

In my heart of hearts I know I should stay away, and I tried. I managed for an entire day after we returned from the tour, but then walking down the street, seeing the hardware store, movement took over before my brain could stop it.

Now, I'm standing outside her apartment, a backpack ready, in my old worn hiking boots. The familiar guilt stabs at me. I can't keep descending down the cliff of this uncontrollable desire. I know I've got to repress it, lock it up and then toss the motherfucker to the bottom of the ocean. Except my poor hopeless heart takes over and reasons that whatever happened in the past have nothing to do with what's happening right now, that I'm not responsible for my parents' actions.

Why should I rob myself of happiness?

"Hi," she greets me with a bright smile.

My gaze traces the curve of her face, and the fall of her hair under the black knit cap she's wearing. I lean in and brush my lips against hers. She looks even better in her tight leggings and fitted coat than she does in her jeans and t-shirts. The outline of her legs remind me of when they were wrapped around my waist. I usher her into the car before I let that train of thought run off its tracks.

"Ready?"

"Yep."

She climbs in, practically bouncing. "I never get to go hiking anymore. Thankfully, Jacob who also works at the shop, agreed to cover for me."

I pull out onto the road and head out of town. "Does he have a crush on you?"

She laughs. "Not one bit. He's the silent type, nice guy though. Are you jealous or something?"

"Definitely jealous," I answer truthfully and glance at her for a beat. "Just want to know if I have any competition."

"Oh..." her blushing is pink perfection, a genuine sweetness I've been craving. "So where are we headed?"

I turn my attention back to the road. "Waterfall hike. I figure it's close, a pretty easy hike, in case you need to get back for your brothers or anything."

"That's very considerate, especially considering how much of a jerk Rueben has been to you."

"I'm not worried about him." I risk another peek at her, she's staring at me slack jawed. "He's just trying to protect his little sister. It's natural, and I don't blame him."

She snorts. "Well, I do."

A fresh wave of guilt assaults me, and I grip the steering wheel tighter. If keeping my distance doesn't work, I have to think of some other plan. At the very least, she'll have to learn the truth about me, about what my parents did. But I can't bring myself to tell her and watch the bright-eyed looks she gives me fade away.

I'll tell her. Just not today.

We make it to the trails, and I'm happy the parking lot is empty. More privacy with her is a good thing. The trail I want to walk on has one waterfall in a little canyon and is about two miles of scenic strolling. I hope she won't be offended, thinking I picked something easy for her.

But she walks beside me, exclaiming over flowers, animals, and other terrain we pass. Her gasp when we reach the waterfall is pure heavenly music.

After she looks her fill and snaps a few photos, I lead her to a small picnic area and with a flourish set my backpack on the table.

"What's in there?" she asks, tentatively, a smile curving her full pink lips.

I walk around the table and straddle the bench beside her. She doesn't fight when I pull her fingers into my hands, cup them to my face and breathe warm air onto her digits.

When I glance up, her eyes are round and wide as she watches me warm each finger until they don't feel as icy. The moment stretches between us, and I want to kiss her but hold myself back. I let myself go when we were at her apartment. Now, I need to be methodical. Get to know her and let her get to know me in return. Otherwise, how will she trust me when things start to unravel?

I clear my throat and jerk the bag down flat. "I didn't bring just any pack. I brought fluffernutter sandwiches and animal crackers."

A laugh pops out of her like one bright peel of a car

horn. "I don't think I've ever had a fluffernutter sandwich. Let's see whatcha got!"

I dig out the food, then the water, and spread it on the table for us. She tucks in, and I let pride at the sight sink into my bones.

Wow, she's beautiful.

I realize I'm staring and focus on my own sandwich. "So how long have you wanted to be a singer?"

She blinks and looks over at me above the brown crust pressed to her lips. Once she swallows, she answers. "I guess since I was little. I've always loved music. My brothers say I used to sing along with my dad to the country songs on the radio, even before I could say the right words."

She glows when she talks about her parents, and suddenly, the food is ash in my mouth.

"You could sing with us when we go to the event, if you wanted." I was going to ask her to anyway. But maybe the guilt pushes me to do it sooner.

"That sounds amazing. I admit, I had so much fun last time. My heart was beating ninety miles a minute, but it was a blast. Do you ever get nervous up there?"

"Every time." I admit.

She stares down into the small bag of animal crackers as she speaks. "I guess, I've just been listening to my brothers tell me how unrealistic my dreams are, and I started to believe it was true. And I'd feel guilty leaving them, so it's easier just to pretend it doesn't matter."

I nod and rub her back through her black coat. "That's understandable. But maybe it's time for them, and you, to accept you need to live your own life for yourself."

Even though I'm saying the words to her, they could easily apply to me. What have I been doing with the band all this time? Building my song portfolio? Yes, but I've been using the band's need for a singer to cling to everything because I fear how much it will all change if I head off to Nashville.

She grabs my hand and cups it between hers. "Thank you. I know we only know a little about each other, but I feel like you understand."

I gently remove stray hairs from her face. "I think you were born to sing. It was obvious to anyone with eyes the other night. I bet if your brothers could see you sing, they'd know it's what you were meant to do."

She huffs out a laugh. "You're just saying that to get in my pants."

It's a joke, but I don't let her laugh it off. I turn her cheek so I can meet her eyes head-on. "No, I mean it, I wouldn't lie to you to give you false hope. You're an amazing singer, and you already have a natural charisma that any performer would kill for. You'll make it, if you give it a try."

She resumes eating, a small smile playing across her lips, her eyes bright and shiny. "Were you serious about letting me sing with the band? Won't they mind you just bringing a stranger?"

I shrug. "The only person who will pretend to mind is Coby, just because she resists change like it's going to set her on fire."

Millie snickers. "I don't know your songs though."

Which reminds me. I flip open my backpack again and dredge up a notebook, the serrated edge still sporting little paper tails. I hand it to her. Nerves roil up in the pit of my stomach. Shit. I'm nervous. When was the last time I was nervous around a woman?

Never.

I suck in a deep breath, calming my nerves. "Um...

Well... I wrote a song for you... I mean for us to sing when we are at the venue."

She blinks and then snatches the notebook. With a smile, she flips it open. I watch her carefully as she reads, monitoring every flicker of her response to it.

I can recite the words to her. I wrote them while thinking of her.

With one touch you entered my soul,
As if your own body were its key,
Not a thing of metal nor gold,
Yet a sensation of love that came,
Through fingertips and eyes,
Through your steady breaths,
Through your sweet words,
And the resolution of my survival self,
To never let anyone sit at my core,
Surrendered in that fleeting moment...

When she finishes, she stares up at me. "It's beautiful. It's a duet, right?"

I nod, not trusting my voice to come out even with the admiration shining so brightly on her face.

"The words are beautiful, and I'd be honored to sing it with you."

I finally wrestle myself under control and gently take back the notebook. "I'm not quite done with the arrangement. When the band practices next, we'll work on it together. With your work schedule, I figure you can't get away so I'll send you a rough recording as we go through it so you can hear how it all sounds together."

She gives me one sharp nod like it's settled and polishes off the last of her food. "Since we're on the subject of work, we should get back soon. I'm sure my brothers are mutinous."

The light is getting low, since we are still technically in winter, the sun still sets early, and the clocks haven't moved forward. "You're right. Better to keep your brothers on my good side while I can."

She snickers, gathers our trash, and tosses it while I repack the bag.

We head out on the trail toward the parking lot, stopping less to marvel this time. Well, she doesn't. I'm watching her as I follow, with a focus she'd probably find uncomfortable. I'm trying to memorize every line of her. Keep her for myself as long as possible.

Because once the world gets ahold of Millie, they won't give her back.

11

MILLIE

Getting ready for work the next day is peaceful. I feel refreshed, like I haven't felt in a long time. It occurs to me that maybe…just maybe…I've been working a little too much, and all these breaks I've been taking with Tyler are good for me.

I doubt my brothers will feel the same way, but I resolve to put days off on the calendar and actually use them. The store won't die if it closes now and then. Hell, maybe Rueben needs a day or two off as well, and then maybe he won't say things that make me want to murder him.

I tie up my hair in a ponytail, grab my jacket and keys, and bounce down to the sidewalk.

But it's not only softly muted morning light that greets me, it's also my two scowling brothers. They're standing on the curb, as if they've been standing in the cold for a while.

"What are you guys doing here? You could have come up and knocked. Or hell, you both have keys to my door." I laugh and shake my head, not that I would have been comfortable with them entering my place without me there, which they've done before, and it pissed me off. At least they learned. Sometimes they're adorable idiots.

Neither of them joins me in a smile. "What's going on now? If this is another intervention about my dating life, I'll warn you now..."

Rueben starts things off. "You didn't come home until late last night, and you weren't answering our calls or texts."

I didn't come home until...

I cross the sidewalk and glare up at them. "Are you kidding me? Have you two been spying on me? I'm pretty sure that's called stalking, and it's a crime."

David matches my irate tone. "Not if the person in question is your baby sister dating random men and coming home at all hours."

"All hours? All hours? It was like seven pm. The store was still open, for fuck's sake. And need I remind you I'm twenty-four years old, which means I can come home whenever I like. You don't get a say in that."

They both glower at me now, and I give them the same face right back. I might not have the stature, the weight, or the beards, but they damn sure don't scare me. Because if I back down now, they'll keep me locked up for the rest of my life, and I'm only now getting my first taste of freedom. I'm not ready to give it up.

"He's not who you think he is, Millie. I told you to stay away from him. Can't you just trust me and listen?" Some of the anger has bled from his voice, but I'm not falling for it.

"Tell me why. Give me one good reason other than you're afraid of your little sister going on a date." I stand there, Wonder Woman pose in place, and I wait.

Both of them just look at me and say nothing. Silence. Pure fucking silence.

"Really? You can't give me a single good reason to trust your judgement about Tyler? Nothing? You are unbelievable. It's been a couple of weeks since I met him, and he's been nothing but a gentleman. And you—you're standing here talking about him like he's the worst sort of person, and then you give me no reason to justify yourselves."

I'm screaming at my big brothers on the sidewalk in the middle of town, and I can't bring myself to care. Not when they deserve it and more.

"You know what, from now on, neither of you gets to comment on my dating life, or I'll be out the door and gone, for good."

Rueben sucks in a breath. "You wouldn't dare. You're a partner in the store, you'd give that all up for one guy you barely know?"

I match his glower with my own. "I wouldn't give it up for some guy, no, but I'd give it up to maintain my freedom. My dignity. To not be treated like some baby to be coddled and locked away."

David's turn to strike a blow. "If you don't want to be treated like a child, then stop acting like one."

"How?" I wave around wildly. "Tell me how I'm acting like a child. I'm not the one stalking my sibling and making threats to get her to stop seeing someone."

I'm breathing heavily, and fog is gusting around me after each exhale. My heart is pounding so hard, it's vibrating in my ears. I need to calm down before I do something, or say something, I can't take back.

"I'm going out of town with Tyler and his band for two days."

"No." David snaps his beanie off his head and drags a hand through his hair. "You can't do that."

"Are you forbidding me?" I challenge.

"Yes," he answers, his tone curt.

"Well guess what, big brother, I can go away with Tyler and I will. The only reason I'm telling you is because I don't want you guys sending a search party after me."

"It's not happening," David says as if the conversation is over.

I snort in annoyance and frustration. "You know what. I think we need a minute. I'm not coming to work today. You can deal with the shop."

Rueben glares. "No, you can't just do that."

"What are you guys? The 'you can't do that' twins?" I drag my phone from my jacket pocket, hit a speed dial button, and wait. Rueben's phone rings and he huffs as he fishes it from the pocket of his red flannel shirt. "Nice, Millie, really?"

When he doesn't answer, I call him until he does and barks, "What?"

"I'm fucking calling off work. Get the hell away from my apartment."

Usually, I'd tell them where I'm going, so they don't worry. This time, I'll let them stew for a bit. I stalk off down the sidewalk, anger simmering through me in a way it rarely does. Only my brothers can drive me to this extreme rage.

Almost immediately, the guilt creeps in, settling between my shoulder blades. But I won't give in, not this time, and not any time they think they have a say in who I can or can't date.

I walk until my feet start to ache in my sneakers, and then I call Jess to come and get me. As long as I'm out of their line of sight, and my point is made, I don't care.

She picks me up and takes me back to her place. It's a small apartment in a complex past the one big box store the zoning board let in to the vicinity of our little picturesque town.

She's decorated it in purples and navy blues to offset the white walls her landlord won't allow her to paint.

It's still morning, so Jess makes us mimosas and we settle on the dove gray couch in her living room. "Tell me everything."

I huff out a long breath and settle into the cushions. "Well, my brothers ambushed me about my personal life, again. They keep acting like Tyler is waiting in the wings to make me a notch on his bedpost."

"Is he?"

I roll my eyes and shove her shoulder. "No, Jess, come on."

"But do you want him to?"

"Want him to what?"

She sips her drink and gives me a knowing look over the rim. "You've been a virgin a long time. There haven't been many guys in your life that your brothers haven't scared away. If he's not running, I say take him to bed, lose your virginity, and celebrate, because he's beautiful. Make him a notch in your bedpost."

I can't help the smile that spreads across my face. "Stop it, you're ridiculous. I don't have bedposts. I don't need notches. I won't lie, I've thought about what spending more time with him means, but I haven't gone all the way there in my imagination, yet. I guess I don't know what all the way there looks like."

Jess snorts. "We saw our first porno together when we were teenagers. I know you know what all the way looks like."

A wash of heat flashes into my cheeks. I'd forgotten about that. It had disturbed me enough to never look at porn again. "Well, let's hope whatever happens between Tyler and me doesn't look like the 70s era Joy of Sex."

We spend a good minute laughing over that until our drinks are gone and my belly aches from her jokes.

Then we get refills, order pizza for lunch, and sit out on her balcony. She's unusually quiet as she props her feet onto the railing.

"What are you thinking about? Do you think I should sleep with him?"

Her look is answer enough. "I think you should do whatever makes you happy. Furthermore, you should call off work more often. We haven't done this in ages, and I'm realizing now how much I miss spending time with you. Just laughing and talking."

She's right. We hang out, of course, but usually only late in the evenings after work when I'm already exhausted. "I'm sorry. Why didn't you say anything?"

"Whenever I ask you to hang out you tell me you're working, going to work, or covering for someone else who should be at work. I know the business is important to you, but you need to find something that isn't all about that store. And I think Tyler is the perfect recipe to get you to enjoy your life more."

Jess always has a knack for calling me on my bullshit. I'm surprised she didn't do it sooner.

"I'm sorry, Jess. I'll make more of an effort to be a better friend. I love you; you know that."

She throws her arm around my shoulders and pulls me into her. I almost topple off the wrought-iron chair right into her. "I love you, too."

A chuckle slips out of me. "Well, the mimosas are working at least. Glad we could have this little heart to heart."

When the pizza arrives, we switch to water and enjoy the pepperoni and banana pepper combo our local pizzeria is known for.

In two days, I'll be out of town, really out of town, for the first time. It makes me appreciate my home all the more.

12

TYLER

Part of me is surprised to have her standing next to me in a little hotel room. Surprised and excited. I can't wait to show her how much fun the band has on tour. Show her the crowds, the dancing, the music. All the things she'll love as much as I do. The other part of me reminds me I'm skating on thin ice and I have a dirty little secret.

She throws her bag on top of one of the queen-size beds and smiles at me. "I considered we might be sharing a room, but it's really sweet you made sure I got my own bed."

I drag her into my arms and kiss her lips, her chin, her throat, and back up to her mouth. She quivers in my hold, and I revel in it, this music playing through her body. "I want you to be comfortable. If you want to sleep in my bed, I won't say no, but I wanted you to have that choice, not force it."

She wraps her arms around my neck and kisses me in earnest this time. I have to stoop to comfortably reach her mouth, but I don't even care, not when she tastes like lemon lime soda and peppermint gum.

We break apart a minute later, and she presses her forehead to my chest. "I don't know what I want yet. I'm sorry."

"You have nothing to apologize for."

I hold her close as she speaks. "All my life, my brothers have been drilling into me that boys only want one thing from me. When I was old enough to date, they would take one look at the pair of them and take off running. It basically meant I stayed single. Dating was just never worth the hassle of dealing with them."

"And is it now?"

She snorts. "I'll be honest, I don't know. They've gotten good at cornering me and forcing me to listen to their opinions."

I cup her head and tease my fingers through her hair relishing the soft sighs she lets out at as I trail my fingers through its length. "Did you ever consider maybe they're so protective of you because of your mutual loss? You're all young and suffered a lot when you were even younger. Maybe they just fear losing you and try to keep you close."

"I know where they're coming from. It's just when they go off about me dating you, I sort of shut down and go into defense mode."

I tilt her chin up with my thumb. "Maybe try not to be so hard on them. I can tell they love you."

If the look on her face is anything to go by, neither of us can believe I'm the one defending her brothers. I let her pull from my arms and explore the room while I watch her until a loud pounding drags us from the room.

We have a show to perform. As usual, we get ready at the venue, this time Millie is with us as we warm up and go over the song list one last time. I love the sense of wonder which settles across her face as she takes it all in.

When the band heads out on stage, she stays in the

wings watching, dancing, and singing. And I sing every song for her. As we queue up the last number, I wave her out to join me. At first, she shakes her head and waves me off, but then I drag her out to the microphone, and she smiles.

She only resists because she doesn't want to encroach on the band and our time to play. Our creative connection takes over. We sing the song I wrote for her like we'd sang it a hundred times, thousands of times before.

And when the curtain falls, the crowd's cheers roar in our ears. But, for a second, it's just Millie and me in our own little bubble. Everything snaps back when the guys circle us, hugging, and jump up and down. Another sold out show, another success. We are on our way.

I hug everyone back, including Millie. We head to the VIP backstage area to celebrate. As usual, we get mobbed by fans and spend a moment signing the merch the venue sells for us while we play. Then I tug Millie to a dark corner and kiss her until she can only cling to me to keep herself upright.

Coby pelts my back with pretzels. "Ugh. Get a room."

When we pull apart, Millie is bright-eyed and breathless. And I can't stop looking at her. Weeks of pent up desire flares to the surface. I want her with every part of me. I don't know what it is about her, maybe it's the way nothing else matters when we're together. But no rush. I'll wait until she's ready.

She grabs a snack of her own and a soda. As usual, I stick to water. "Ready to get out of here?" I ask with a jerk of my chin to the door.

She holds my gaze for a beat and then hers drops to my mouth before she looks back up at me. "Back to our room."

Four little words have me heated in certain spots. It's not

a question, more so an invite but still, I want to make sure we're on the same page. "If that's what you want."

Her mouth curves in a small smile. "It is."

The second she sets her can on a nearby table, I grab her hand again and lead her outside. The alley is empty, but we find a cab to take us to the hotel soon enough. Once inside, I tug her jacket from her arms and ditch mine as well, right on the other side of the closed door.

For the briefest moment, a streak of guilt flashes like a warning sign on the highway. *Danger ahead.* Once we cross that bridge, there's no turning back. I should tell her about my parents. But when she presses her mouth to the underside of my jaw in a soft kiss, logic flies out the window, and gives way to the heady sensation of being desired.

Right now I want to taste her mouth, the slow kissing, the passionate kissing, the grinding, biting, feeling each other. I want to lose myself in her.

I pull her against my chest, my heart lurching toward her. "You were incredible tonight," I say, my voice raspy, full of want.

She tugs the hem of my t-shirt toward my shoulder blades as I walk her backward toward the beds. "You too."

Before we go further, I still her hands, capturing them in mine. I want her on the bed and between her legs more than anything, but not if she's not ready for it. "Tell me what you want, Millie."

"What do you want?"

I shake my head. "It's not about what I want, right now. It's you. All for you. Tell me."

She scans my face and steps closer, the heat of her driving my already hard cock into steel.

"I want this." Her green eyes pierce mine. Vulnerability, desire, readiness—that's what I see in her gaze. "I want you."

Every inch of my skin heats up, burning with desire for her. I capture her mouth and lead her back to the bed. When she sits, I follow her down and pull her into my arms again. She's so soft, curves everywhere, the swell of her full breasts teasing me as she presses in tight.

"If at any point you change your mind—" She covers my lips with her hand.

"If I decide I need to stop, I'll say something. And I trust you to listen if I need that. Do you trust me to tell you?"

I nod, her fingers still over my lips. When she nods in return, I lick her finger, and she lets out a squeal and jerks them away. But I don't let her get far, and then we're kissing again. Our tongues stroking in a perfect rhythm.

"How do you make me feel like this?" she asks when we break for air.

My response comes out low and deep. "Like what?"

"Like I'm burning from the inside out." She tugs on my shirt again, and I strip it off and throw it away.

"Your turn."

She swallows heavily, and then I get rid of her shirt. Her bra is peach lace and cups the heavy curve of her breasts like an invitation.

"May I?" I whisper, leaning down.

She nods and I remove the fabric and explore each of her tight pink nipples with my tongue. God, she tastes so good. Slightly salty from sweat, but soft and warm. Her fingers thread into my hair, and I lift my face to catch hers. Meshing our lips together again.

She moans into my mouth, and the sound shoots through me. I'm so hard I can barely think straight. But it doesn't matter. I have to make this good for her. So good for her.

I gently lay her back on the bed, and she smiles as she

watches me trail my mouth down her smooth pale belly to the top of her jeans. Then I strip them off her legs, her underwear, too.

"Not fair, I want you naked, too."

"Fair is fair." I chuckle and quickly get rid of my clothes. When I push off my boxer briefs and my cock springs free, her eyes lock to my length. I catch the surprise look on her face. "Are you okay?"

She licks her lips and nods. "You're just...um...big."

"Don't worry, it'll fit." I bring my hand to my dick and stroke it as she stares. "And if it hurts just say the word and we'll—"

"Stop. I know." She reaches for me. But I don't join her immediately. First, I start at her knees, licking and nipping my way up her thighs to her pussy. She parts for me, with no prompting, and I hum my approval into her skin.

A soft patch of curls tops her wet, slick core. I lean in and run my tongue from her opening to her clit. Her entire body seizes off the bed. The deep moan she emits rakes my control to shreds.

I lap at her flesh until she's wrapping her legs around my shoulders and her hands are clutching at my head. She's moaning long and loud now, arching her hips into my face. Lust slams into me from all corners. She's so fucking wet. So slick. I want to feel her come on my tongue; commit how she tastes into my memory. I increase the pace until she breaks, her body shaking and shuddering until she finally goes limp.

"Wow," she whispers a moment later.

I give her one more lick, carefully climb off her and grab my pants. With a condom in hand, I return to the bed to look at her. She's spread open, her legs splayed, her long hair falls wildly on the covers.

"Do you still want this?" I ask.

She nods and reaches for me. I tear open the condom, roll it on, and climb back between her thighs. She doesn't hesitate to pull my mouth to hers, kissing and nipping at my lips.

I slide against her, and holy fuck; she feels so good. Carefully, I reach between us and notch myself at her opening. She tilts her hips, drawing me in faster than I plan. This is the most exquisite torture. I hiss out a breath and pause, needing a minute to gain control. "You keep doing that, it'll be over in seconds."

"We have all night."

A shudder wracks my body. Fuck. She can't say stuff like this. I press further, and she hisses slightly. When I pause, she shakes her head, clinging to me. "No, please," she begs. "Don't stop."

With her urging, I surge forward, sinking deep. She lets out another heavy exhale and hugs me tight. "I feel so...full."

I chuckle, but when she arches her hips upward, the levity falls away, my mindless pleasure replacing it.

"Please," she begs. And I don't need further instruction. I pull out until the tip of me is at her core, then gently thrust back inside her most sensitive spot. The wet heat of her cups me tight and insistent. So tight I can barely think through it. God, this is what it's like to want someone with every fiber of your being. This desire for her. My balls start to draw up, my orgasm already looming, but I can't go without her.

"Touch yourself," I tell her.

"What?" she asks, her voice wobbly.

I gently guide her hand between us so she can thrum her own little nub while I take her.

She figures out a rhythm quickly, and the moment I feel

the sharp pulse of her pussy squeezing me, I surge into her tight and hard, letting my own orgasm wash over me.

It takes a minute for me to come down from the edge, another to clean up, and soothe her bright pink skin with a warm washcloth.

"Good?" I ask before dusting a kiss on her lips.

"I've never felt better."

I pull back the covers and settle with her underneath. "Me too."

She nestles against me, and I press my lips to her hair. As I hold her and listen to her soft breathing while she sleeps, everything becomes crystal clear. I want Millie to be happy in every way—in bed and out of bed. I want to give her limitless counts of orgasms. I want to see her smile. I want to watch her sing on stage. I want to make her happy... because I've fallen in love with her.

My gut twists. I'll tell her everything tomorrow.

13

MILLIE

The sunlight streaming through the curtains wakes me up. I blink into the light and shift in the warm blankets. Then I realize I'm not alone in bed. Tyler and every naked inch of his long, lean muscles are tucked up against my back. He feels so perfect wrapped around me.

I remember how he took his time last night, making me come twice before I fell asleep on him. It hits me all over again, I'm not a virgin anymore.

I take stock. How do I feel? Different. Like I'm connected to my body for the first time in my life. Every ripple of sensation feels like so much more.

Do I regret making love to Tyler?

Not for a single moment. He was so gentle with me—warm, and caring.

He snores lightly in my ear and I smile, my head on the pillow but his arm underneath my neck. I fear shifting and waking him up. This moment is precious to me, and I want to stay in it a little while longer.

Of course, life always has other plans, and the alarm on

one of our phones blares through the room. He jolts against me and then rockets upward to find the source of the noise.

It's his phone, still in his jeans pocket. After he stops the alarm, he crawls back in bed and tugs my body into the curve of his. "Good morning, Beautiful."

I cover his arms with my own. "Good morning."

"How are you feeling?"

I pull him tighter around me. "I'm not really sure. Weird, I guess. But not in a bad way."

His lips make a trail up my neck to my ear and then around my forehead. He speaks against my skin. "That's okay. As long as you're happy. Are you?"

I tilt my head so I can meet his eyes. "Yes, I'm happy."

"Then that's all that matters. And I don't want you to worry, we'll only ever do what you're comfortable with. If you want to have sex again in the future, we can. If you just want to kiss...it's whatever you want."

Hope bounces in my chest. "We're gonna do this again."

"Only if you want."

"I want."

"Are we like...." my voice trails. I hate that I get so timid around him.

"Boyfriend and girlfriend," he finishes, a smile on his lips. "Dating. I'm fine with whatever label you want to put on us."

My heart leaps with joy. I want to spend the day in bed with him. But I know checkout is in a couple of hours. We need to get the van packed up from the venue last night, and no doubt my brothers will be waiting for me at home.

The rest of the band meets us at the bar. None of them make me feel awkward.. Which makes me feel better—like I'm part of them, like family. It takes a while to break down all the instruments, and they talk me through it as I help.

I'm a little nervous, as I fear destroying something. While I've always been a good singer, I've never really played an instrument outside of the piano.

After we get everything packed, we head to the gas station, cram a few shopping bags full of snacks and drinks, and get on the road. We aren't super far from Cherry Falls, but it takes us several hours to get back to town. We stop at the band's studio first, and I help them unload the vehicle.

Tyler tells me over and over that I don't actually have to help since I'm not part of the band, but it makes me feel silly to sit around while other people are working.

Once everything is put away, the rest of the band heads home.

Tyler drives me back to my house. I glance nervously around the neighborhood. The sidewalk outside my apartment looks clear. He holds open the little door that leads up to my loft, and I walk ahead of him inside.

But as soon as the door closes behind us, I stop dead. David is sitting on the steps. His head is hunched down, his beanie spinning round and round between his hands.

"What are you doing here?" It comes out more forcefully than I expect.

David's head snaps up as he takes in the two of us. Tyler grips my hand and gives me a little squeeze. A silent way of him letting me handle this on my own, and I appreciate it.

David narrows his eyes. "What am I doing here? Waiting for you. You were gone all night, and all day yesterday, I was worried about you. I called your phone, but you didn't answer."

I throw up my hands and shake my head. "What do you expect? I told you guys I was going away with Tyler. That should've been enough for you. In that instance, you should simply tell me you love me, tell me to be careful, and then leave me the hell alone until I call you or reach out in some way. Why is this so difficult for you guys to understand?"

When David shoves off the stairs to lumber down to the landing, Tyler moves to put me behind him, but I don't allow it, meeting my brother chest to chest.

"What else do you have to say?" I demand. "Say it, so you can leave."

David blinks, hurt flashes in his eyes, but I don't back down, not when he's trying to throw me into a cage. "Well, we might have been content to let you do your own thing, but that was until we found out you were sharing a hotel room with a stranger."

I stiffen. "He's not a stranger. He's my boyfriend. And I'm not going to even ask you how you know we shared a room together. It's none of your business. Go home, and get some rest. Maybe, *maybe*, we can talk about this later when you've calmed down and Rueben is equally calm. You keep harping on me acting like an adult, but then you guys treat me like a child, and then act like children yourselves. Following me around, making demands, never explaining yourselves. What am I supposed to do with that?"

My brother shouts in frustration, and I guess Tyler has had enough.

He steps forward in the cramped space and addresses my brother. "I don't know what you know about me, but I care about your sister."

David only glares and sneers at the hand Tyler holds out to shake. "Musicians only care about parties and their next show." He maintains eye contact with Tyler as he speaks to me. "You'll never be able to match the adrenaline for him. He'll get bored and leave you heartbroken. Take my word on it."

I gasp, stalk to the door, and open it wide. "Get out, now. Before we both do something stupid."

David glares between us and stalks out the door. It's not until he's gone that I can suck in a full breath again. I'm so angry, I'm shaking, and tears build up in the corners of my eyes.

Tyler pulls me gently into his embrace. "Baby, it's okay. He's only trying to keep you safe. I'm not going anywhere, and he's not going to scare me off."

I wipe my face on the back of my hand and lead him up to my apartment.

He carries my bag in and places it on my couch.

I survey my home, and it feels dull, drab, lifeless. "I wish I could go on the road like you guys. Be brave and do shows and just live."

He crosses the room and gently cups my face between his big palms, his calloused fingers rubbing across my cheeks. "Then come with us. We're meeting with record execs tomorrow, and I know they're going to offer us a contract. If they do, it means the band will have to move to Nashville. You can come with us. Join the band and live your dreams."

I don't even let the little balloon of hope build in my chest. "Don't you need to ask the band if I can join? Do they get a say in it?"

He shakes his head and pulls me in tighter until his lips are only a few inches from mine. "No. I love them, but if they can't see you're good for us, then they aren't the band I know. Besides, they already feel like you belong with us. Or else they wouldn't have let you touch their instruments. Especially Coby."

Even if his offer sounds, literally, like a dream come true,

I don't know if I can do it. Leave my life, leave my brothers and Jess, to go to Nashville with a man I barely know.

I lay my hands over his, still clutching my face. "I'd have to think about it all. And it's not just my brothers that weigh in my decision. It's my entire life here. I'd be giving up everything."

"But think of what you'll gain."

He makes it sound so easy. Like I'm trading a sub-standard existence for this glamorous life I've only just gotten a taste of.

"It's easy for you because you've been doing this whole thing a while. I don't know what to expect, how it will feel to be away from my brothers. I've never been away from them for more than a day. The one time I went on a high school field trip two towns over, I cried because I got homesick."

"As I told you last night, and this morning, the choice is always yours." He presses his forehead to mine, and I breathe in the spicy scent of him. "You do what you feel comfortable with."

When he kisses me goodbye, I don't want him to go, but I know we probably both need time to process and think.

He leaves, and I throw myself on the couch. In only a few short hours, my entire world has been turned upside down. On one hand, I have my life in Cherry Falls. On the other, the opportunity of a lifetime. I only have to leave my entire world behind to get it.

14

TYLER

The band meets the record execs at a local law office in Rosewood. I've never been inside the building, but it's decorated in stainless steel and shades of gray. It looks barren, like a hotel trying to be trendier than it actually is.

We file into a conference room. The man and woman from the record company take seats across from us at the long mahogany table.

The woman, Talia, speaks first, breaking the tension. "We're so excited to be here talking to you. Can we offer you a drink or a snack?" She waves toward a cart off to the side of the room.

Before we agreed to the meeting, the band decided I'd speak for us. While Clint is here as our manager, I'm the one speaking for us and will ensure we all get what we want out of this deal. I lean across the table and give her a (hopefully) disarming smile. "No, thank you. We'd just like to get down to business, please."

The man, Henry, nods and matches my folded hands on the table's surface. "Of course, we know your time is valuable. We're excited to be here with you, as Talia said, because we've been scouting some of your recent shows. The last one upstate sold out in only a few days. Unheard of for the little bar you played that night."

I nod, hoping he'll get to his point, eventually. We aren't the sort of band who need constant praise. Not that we're cocky, but we know we're good.

Talia silently gets out of her chair, crosses the room, and pours herself some coffee. As she walks back, she addresses us. "Tell us about the new girl you've been playing with. She's not here today."

My mind instantly goes to Millie and realize right away where they're going with this. Their interest in Devil in the Highway lies solely if Millie is a part of the band. I glance over at my bandmates. Cash lifts a shoulder in indifference. Gavin and Coby nod. They're leaving the decision up to me.

"Her name is Millie," I start carefully. "She's my girl-friend. She's not in the band, she's just done a couple songs with me."

"We like her," Henry says, almost conspiratorially. "She gives your sound the folk edge you've been missing for a while. While you've been on our radar for some time, it wasn't until you made this change that we decided to make contact."

I know I shouldn't take offense to his statement, but it still stings. "What do you want from us then?"

Henry and Talia nod at each other. It's almost like they're reading each other's minds. Then Henry takes the lead again. "Tell us how long you've been playing original songs."

On my right, Coby clears her throat. "Only a short time. Before that, we did our own versions of covers. The crowds love it, but by our ticket sales lately, they love our original stuff more. All of which, Tyler writes, while we help with the accompaniment."

"Do you enjoy songwriting?" Henry asks me.

I nod. "I enjoy it. I've had a lot of fun coming up with songs that fit our sound and the way we like to play together."

Like a pair of well-trained hawks, Talia swoops in again. "And your girlfriend, does she write music, too?"

Millie and I hadn't discussed it. We'd gone over the song I wrote for her, but she hadn't been geeking out about the arrangement like I do sometimes. "I don't know, honestly. She enjoys singing the songs I write, but we haven't had the opportunity to work on one together, yet."

I wasn't about to confess how new our relationship is to these people. They look like they are sniffing out weaknesses. We're supposed to trust them with our career, but I can't see how, not like this.

Talia sips her coffee and then offers another of her countless bright sunny smiles. "Well, we hope we can meet Millie while we're in town. And if we stay a little longer to await your decision, then maybe we can look through our client list and see who might benefit from new songs on their rosters. Songs you can write for them."

I walk right in that one. Even I have to give it to them, they're good at their jobs. It took seconds to zone in on my weaknesses and press all the buttons I have. Except my parents, which I'm sure they know is one button too far. But I don't have a doubt in my head they aren't aware of my history from birth until now.

It takes effort to try to match Talia's smile. "I'll have to see if she is available. I'm sure she'd love to meet you guys, too. As you heard, she's a lovely singer, and wants to pursue music herself."

Henry fetches coffee this time with considerably less grace than Talia, having a foot of height and at least a hundred pounds on her. "That's good to hear. If you decide she can't play with your band well, then she'll be free to do as she wishes, including sign with a label on her own."

I can feel Coby bristling from her seat, ready to launch into the conversation. Gavin strokes her arm in an attempt to calm her down, but it likely won't hold for long.

This is my fault. Not that Millie doesn't deserve this opportunity, I brought her in to sing with us. But now, this offer seems contingent upon her becoming a permanent member.

It's something we'll need to discuss as a group, but not while these guys are breathing down our necks waiting for any answer. Talia and Henry know how to read an audience. They don't linger, promising to reach out for an answer soon. They leave us in their fancy conference room to talk things out amongst ourselves.

I swivel in the chair to face my friends. "What do you guys think?"

Coby shifts in her chair, the leather of her jacket creaking as her arms flex. I wait her out, and she doesn't hold out long. "I like her okay, but this is our chance, and now, it's dependent on someone we don't know very well."

We've been friends long enough for me to read her. I can tell she's worried I'll get upset, but I understand. I don't want any of them to resent me for bringing her around, because the band won't withstand that.

"We have to decide as a band," I say to my friends. "We've been together for a few years. If you guys don't want me to ask Millie, then we don't."

Cash speaks up next. "I mean, do we want to pin our career on a girl you're sleeping with?"

His comment gets under my skin. I clench my fists and

shake my head. "It's not just sex. I'm falling in love with her. I don't plan to let her go anytime soon."

It feels good to admit out loud. Even if the first time I do, it should have been to her. They all stare at me now, equal looks of concern spread between them.

Coby is the one who brings up the obvious. Painful, but obvious. "If it's not just sex, then you've told her about your parents right?"

Cash and Gavin glance between us. Damn. She always did know how to get me right through the heart. "I haven't told her yet, but I'm planning on it."

"Planning?"

I nod. "Planning, yes. I can't just spring it on her when I tell her about all of this."

Coby shoves out of the chair and starts pacing the carpet behind her. "You should have told her the second you realized it."

What can I say to reassure them? It isn't really them I need to comfort. But I feel compelled to, after the news we just got.

Cash cuts in. "Not to break things up here, but it's pretty obvious that without Millie we don't have a contract. No record. No Nashville. None of it."

A sharp wedge of guilt lodges under my ribs. "And when I tell Millie the truth, that my parents killed hers all those years ago, I might lose her all together."

15

———

MILLIE

My brothers leave me alone for a day. But they must have been planning some kind of intervention. When I head up my stairs after my work shift, my door is unlocked, and they're both sitting in my apartment. Rueben on the couch, David leaning against the wall by the windows.

I lock the door behind me and let my keys hit the table with a clatter. "If this is another attempt for you to make decisions for me and assume I'll follow them, I'm not in the mood."

My hands are already on my hips and my glare is in place. We haven't had a civil conversation in days, and I'm so over it. "Say what you need to say, and get out."

Rueben frowns heavily and rubs his hands down his jean-clad thighs. "Since you know why we're here, I won't bother explaining. Neither of us approve of how you stayed in the hotel with that man."

"That man's name is Tyler, and it's really none of your business. Why do I keep having to repeat that?"

I notice David is quiet in the corner, grinding his teeth

together, no doubt to keep us from having another shouting match.

Rueben continues, "You will stop seeing him, or I won't give you any more hours at the store."

My anger had already been at a low simmer when I found them in my apartment. Now, it blazes through me, a full-on inferno. Who the hell does he think he is? "Well, you can cut my hours, but you'll still be paying me since I own 50% of the store, and legally, you're required to. If you want me to stay home and not work for my money, fine."

The surprised blink he gives me tells me easily he wasn't expecting me to push back.

"Anything else?" I ask.

"You'd give up the store?"

"No, you're trying to take it from me. There's a difference. And I throw out an ante. If you two keep pushing me on this, you're going to lose me. I'll leave this town for good, and you won't see me again."

David shoves off the wall and surges toward me. "You'd give up your family for some guy."

"No, I'd give up my unsupportive, judgmental family, because they pushed me out of their lives. Again, these are your decisions to make."

"And just where are you going to go?" Rueben demands, standing by David so they can both tower over me.

"Anywhere. That's the best part about meeting this guy. He actually believes me capable of anything I want. For the first time, I feel like I have options. Even if he and I don't stay together, now, I know there's a world out there, and I don't intend to stay here in a pretty convenient cage."

Rueben sets his jaw and exchanges a look with David. "We only want you to be safe."

"Then let me live my life. Safety is a worthless commodity when it becomes captivity."

I wait for them to drag things out more, but David nudges Rueben's elbow, and they both stalk out the door, slamming it as they head down the stairs.

When they go, I slump on the couch and let out a long sigh. Tears slip down my cheeks, and I scrub them away. I hate that we're fighting so much about my relationship of all things, but they're being unreasonable. Why can't they just let me face this—ride it out, or screw it up on my own?

I pick up my phone and call Tyler. It rings several times and then shifts to voicemail. I hang up before it beeps and call Jess who picks up on the second ring.

"Whatup? Ready to tell me about your trip?"

I roll my eyes. "Let's go to the bar. I need a drink and some talk time. My brothers are being fucking obnoxious about Tyler and my staying at the hotel with him."

She squeals aloud, and I can hear her throwing things in the background. "I need to know everything so get your stuff, and meet me there now."

I laugh at her and hang up. No one is going to see me tonight, so I grab my purse, my keys, and head back out the door in my jeans and t-shirt from work.

The bar is a quick walk from my place. She takes a bit longer to arrive since she's coming from the edge of town. Once we're settled at the bar, beers in hand, she demands to know everything.

Of course, I'm not about to give her a play-by-play, but I share the highlights. "We played a show, and I sang a song with him. Then we had an afterparty. But we didn't stay for long and went back to our hotel room. And yes, we had sex."

She squeals again, loud enough the other patrons glance

over at us. I shush her with my hands, trapping hers under mine. "Calm down. It's not the end of the world."

"Are you okay? Did he make sure everything was okay?"

I nod, heat washing up my cheeks and around my ears. "Yes, it was wonderful. He was sweet and gentle."

She shares some of her dating war stories, the highs and lows of her sex life that I've heard over and over. When we leave the bar, I'm a little tipsy. Jess, as the designated driver, stopped drinking long before.

"Where to Madam?" she asks as we slide inside her car.

I give her a grin. "Do you mind driving me to Rosewood? Tyler lives there."

Her laugh echoes around the mostly deserted main street. She taps the GPS to life. "Address?"

I recite it to Jess. Tyler had given me his address a while back, and I hoped I wouldn't be surprising him by showing up out of the blue.

About half an hour later, we pull in front of Tyler's townhouse. I spot his black truck right away. Excitement courses through my veins. My heart beats faster, blood rushes to my face, and ah, down there.

"You're good here?" Jess asks.

I nod. "Thanks, Jess. You can go, I'll be fine. And text me when you get home."

"Be safe, okay."

"Always."

I slide out of the car, wave her goodbye. Then I walk over to his door. I take a deep breath then I knock on his apartment, and he answers, shirtless.

"Are you okay? What's going on?"

Pulsating with need, I shove into his apartment and drag his mouth to mine. He hesitates for a moment and then kisses me deeper.

When I stumble and break the kiss, he catches me up in his arms and carries me to his couch. "Are you okay?"

I nod, listing to the side. "Great. Jess and I were just out."

He goes rigid beside me. "You're drunk."

"You're drunk," I counter. Maybe this is a bad idea. I should have gone home and slept some of the booze off before I saw him. There may be several rounds of beer and liquor in my gut, but I can tell he's angry.

He stalks back to a hallway and returns with his clothes on now, jeans, and a black t-shirt. His keys in his hand. "I'm taking you home. You need to drink water and take some Tylenol. It'll help for tomorrow."

My shoulders droop. I poke my head over the arm of his furniture. "Why do all the men in my life think I can't take care of myself?"

"You're drunk, so obviously you can't at the moment. How did you get here? Did you drive? Take a Lyft while drunk?" His tone is chiding, and it burns through me.

"I'm a goddamn adult. I can drink with my friend if I want to."

After he grabs a jacket for himself, he leads me down to his car. I don't speak, mostly so I can focus on keeping the world from spinning around me. But also, because I can't believe how much he's acting like my brothers right now.

We get into his car, and he heads back toward town. He breaks the silence first. "You, of all people, should know the dangers of drunk driving. I'm just stunned."

I wave out the window, my head leaning into the seatbelt. "Did you see my car outside your house? No. My girlfriend Jess dropped me here. Besides, my car still isn't working from the last time it broke down with you. My parents were killed by a drunk driver, Tyler. Why would I ever be so thoughtless?"

He huffs and resettles in the driver's seat. His posture is easier now as I glance at him from the corner of my eyes. So, he's upset because he thought I put myself in danger? It doesn't make the sting at how he spoke to me any less.

We get to my place, and he leads me up to my apartment. When we get inside, I clean up, put on pajamas and lay in bed. He comes in after a while with a glass of water for me to drink.

"I'm sorry I spoke to you like that. You're right. You're an adult and can make your own choices."

"I shouldn't have come to your place unannounced and not fully myself."

"You can come to me anytime."

"Do you want to—" I lean in and try to kiss him, but he gently tugs my hands from his face.

"Get some rest. We can talk things out in the morning."

The rejection stacks on top of the hurt from his tone, building a leaning tower of pity in my gut. I lay down on the bed and turn my back to him. It takes a while before he strips off his clothes and crawls into the bed with me.

Lying beside him, I'm so very aware of every inch of his warm body under the covers beside mine. Need for him thrums through my blood, but I don't bother trying to touch him. Not when he's going to push me away again.

The tears fall quietly, and at some point, I slip into a hazy doze.

16

TYLER

I wake before her, even before the sun rises, but I can't bring myself to get out of bed. Not when she's so soft and warm against me. She feels so good, so right in my arms. Absurdly, I think I can't possibly let her go. Which means, I need to tell her the truth, as soon as possible. Any longer, and I risk her walking away forever. Hell, I've already risked it.

It's not even about the contract. I don't care about it. I only care that she doesn't hate me when she learns the truth.

I don't know how long I lay there, my brain spinning things around in my head over and over. By the time she wakes up and looks at me with a smile, I'm wound so tight all I can do is climb out of the bed and head to the kitchen.

A few minutes later, she follows me out. "Are you okay?"

I shake my head and start the coffee. But a lie escapes easier than the truth right now. "I'm fine. Just give me a minute to get going."

She stiffens in the corner of my vision and then goes to

sit on the couch, her pink floral robe tucked tight around her.

Once the coffee is finished, I'm a little more firmly on solid ground. I make us both a cup and join her on the couch. Her big green eyes are wide and concerned and it kills me that I've made her worry. She probably thinks I'm still upset about last night.

I wrap her hands around her cup and take mine, using it as a barrier between us, needing the distance. "This is going to be an abrupt question, but humor me, do you know anything about your parents' car accident?"

She freezes as she raises her mug to her lips, and then gently draws it back down to rest on the top of her knees. "Why do you ask?"

"Please, just tell me."

She blinks at the rawness of my tone. "No, my brothers never told me anything about it. They think they're protecting me. When I was younger, I considered looking up the information on my own, but it felt like betraying them, so I never did. And then, as I grew older, I decided I really didn't need to know everything. The fact is they're gone. Nothing can bring them back."

Needing to confess my sins, I swallow the lump clogging my throat, take another drink, and set the cup on the table. It can't save me now. "What I'm about to say might be a lot. So just let me finish, okay?"

She lifts my chin to meet my eyes. "You're scaring me. Just say whatever you need to say."

"I should explain a few things first. My parents weren't good people. Well, they took care of me when they weren't drinking. But as I got older, the sober times were rarer than the times they were drunk. Worse, when they drank, they liked to use me as a punching bag. My Gramps' house was the only safe place I had. I spent more time with him as a kid than them, which I guess made things easier after they died."

"I'm sorry."

Her hand curls around my forearm. Support. She wants to support me. Doubt emerges and tries to consume me, but I shove it down. I have to keep going, get it all out so we can get through it.

"Well, they drank a lot, especially that last year. Then one night, they got drunk, climbed behind the wheel of their car and they crashed into another car. Everyone involved died, both my parents and the two people in the other vehicle."

My voice cracked on the end, and she grips me tighter. "That's why you were upset last night. Why you got angry at the thought of me drinking and driving."

Still, she's only thinking about me. I gently peel her hand from my arm so I can stand up, move around. If I sit with my thoughts, they turn into loathing, pity.

"Yes, that's why I got upset. It wasn't about you. I trust you, and I know you make good choices. My reaction was more about me. And I'm sorry for lashing out at you for it."

Her brows furrow. "I understand now."

Does she?

I turn to look at her now. There's no way I can repeat myself to drag it all out again and admit the truth to her. But I have to. I need to. I take a deep breath and say the words that are bottled up inside me. "My parents were driving on Route 220 when they crashed into another car, right off the Cherry Falls exit."

"Tyler." Her voice is a shaky whisper as the slow dawning horror creeps across her face.

"It happened thirteen years ago," I continue, hating myself for hurting her.

Her skin pales, and tears build up in her eyes. "My parents?" she whispers.

I can only nod, hanging my head, the shame too heavy to bear.

She wraps her arms around her knees and draws them up into her chest. I want to comfort her, but the second I take a step closer she shakes her head, pressing into the arm of the couch.

Her voice is stronger now but no less cutting. "You knew? How long? For how long?"

I cement my cowardice and face the windows, so I don't have to see the tears sliding down her cheeks. "I figured it out after our first date when you spoke about your parents. I left our date that night and went to my Gramps who told me everything."

"You've known for a while."

I shove my fingers into my hair. "Yes."

She lets out a sob, and I turn back, rushing to her side, but she shoves me away. "No. Don't you dare touch me right now. You knew this whole time. You knew when we slept together. You—"

I whip back around to look at her. She sits erect, the tension in every line of her body.

"I just wanted..."

"Wanted what?" She cuts me off, her voice vibrating with fury. "You slept with me. I gave you my virginity." She stops and closes her eyes for a beat before opening them again, her gaze sharp as a blade. "I trusted you."

My heart drops. She's slipping out of my reach and there's nothing I can do. The whole thing makes me feel sick to my soul.

"You should leave," she says coldly.

Weighted down by so many emotions, I stand, go into the room, dress quickly, and come back out. "I'll go. I can see you don't want me here now. Please know I wasn't trying to hurt you by keeping it from you. I just didn't want to lose you, so I made excuses and told myself I'd tell you when it was the right time."

She doesn't say a word as I walk out the door. Her brothers are standing on the curb when I reach the ground level. They take one look at my face, glare, and storm up the stairs into her apartment.

At least she won't be alone. It's all the comfort I can give her right now. I don't get more than a step before David comes back out the door. It slams loudly into the wall. "Get back in here. We aren't done yet."

I don't fight it, even knowing she wanted me to leave. David leads me back inside. Rueben is sitting next to her. She's shifted, so she's leaning on the back of the couch now, her arms still around her knees.

"What did you say to her?" David demands.

I drag a hand through my hair. "I told her the truth."

Rueben mutters, "Fuck."

It's enough to gain her attention, and she shifts on the couch to look between her brothers.

"You both knew about this?"

Shit. I thought they hated me because I was dating their sister. Not once did I stop to consider they hate me because of the same reasons I feared she eventually would. It makes perfect sense. They would have had access to the medical reports and investigations after everything happened. My name would stand out to them easily enough.

When they don't answer, she screams at them. "How long did you know he was their son?"

Rueben answers for them both. "I realized the moment he told me his name in the hardware store. The day he came back to ask you out that first time."

She glares between us all now. "Why? What have I done to make you all so comfortable lying to me? Or wait...is this more macho protecting me bullshit? Because leaving out pertinent information regarding my life doesn't count as protection. It's a dick move, from all of you."

"We're sorry. We really didn't know how to tell you," David says, voice solemn. "You know how hard it is for us to talk about Mom and Dad. Plus, you were happy, even if we were all fighting a lot. Even if we basically stalked you for this entire relationship just waiting for this fucking moment to occur. It was the reason we didn't want you to see him. We knew, eventually, this would come out, either you would figure it out, or he would tell you, and you'd get hurt."

She threw her hands up and storms across the room toward her kitchen for a tissue. "Well, I wouldn't be nearly as hurt if someone would have taken it upon themselves to treat me like a fucking adult."

I clench my hands and wait. No point in going until she's vented all her fury on us equally. Inside, I'm dying. It's almost like I don't even get a proper goodbye. Our last kiss was the sloppy drunk one she gave me last night.

Regret slashes through me. I won't get to feel her arms around me again. Or smell her hair in the morning when I wake up beside her. Losing those things is worse than any other loss I've suffered.

It's in that moment, that heartbreaking moment, I realize, I'm in love with her.

She waves toward the door. "Just get out, all of you. I don't want to see you for a while. Not until I wrap my head around everything."

We all file out into the hall and down to the sidewalk. I stop to meet her brother's gazes. "For what it's worth, I'm sorry. I love her and would never have hurt her. And as for my parents, I'm sorry they caused you so much loss. They deserved their fate, yours didn't."

Neither says a word. I don't expect them to. Stuffing my hands in my pockets I walk toward my car to get away as fast and as far as possible.

17

MILLIE

I should be at work. But even as the thought passes through my brain, it blows away, carried on an unseen wind, and I go back to not caring about anything.

It's been three days since my brothers, and Tyler, blew my world apart. When I let myself focus on it for too long, grief and anger threaten to swamp me all over again. So I stay in bed, I eat snatches of toast in between rounds of tears.

Am I crying because I lost my parents? Or that I'm upset at my brothers for not trusting me enough to tell me the truth? I don't know. All I know is, it feels like I've lost Tyler too, which seems infinitely fresher and more unbearable right now.

My phone rings every few hours between Tyler calling, my brothers, and Jess. I know they're all worried about me, but caring feels too hard, like too much to bear.

Later in the evening, my brothers knock on the door, their heavy pounding dragging me out of sleep. I answer it, and David silently hands me a box of food, French toast, if the scent of cinnamon is to be believed.

I shake my head, but he puts it into my hand and, only then, allows me to close the door in his face.

It's not the lying, well mostly. It's the fact that every single one of them made this decision for me, like they knew what was best for me, an adult with her own life, her own hopes, her own dreams.

Rueben calls as I shove a piece of French toast in my mouth. Eating is difficult, it feels foreign and unappealing as I chew and swallow. Like I'm watching myself do these things instead of participating, and it's easier that way.

I finish the French toast, my belly pleasantly full for the first time in a few days. As if finally given permission, I sort of come out of a fog. I'm stiff, I need a shower, and I'm still so mad at all the men in my life I could smack them, but letting myself wallow, even for a short time helped.

I clean my apartment and take a shower so I can go see my best friend. While absolutely insane, she always has good insight into why my brothers do the stupid things they do. And she has far more experience with men than I do.

Tyler's expression, as he left the other day, looked absolutely tortured, and it's been haunting me since that morning. For some reason, it feels worse than my brothers. Yes, they betrayed me, but I'll always have them no matter what. Tyler isn't a certainty in my life. A harsh reality the other day forced me to face that head on.

Jess doesn't ask questions, and she doesn't demand answers when I show up at her little apartment with my hair still wet and in a messy bun. My brothers must have called her.

"I was five minutes from saddling the horses and riding to your rescue. Are you okay?" she asks, still hugging me in her open doorway.

I nod. And it's mostly true. "I feel wrung out. Like I've

reached the end of my emotional rope, and one more thing is going to leave me plummeting to my death."

She grabs a bottle of wine and sits me down on her couch. "Then let's get you a safety line for that climb."

The sight of the alcohol does something to me now. It's not physical, but it almost just hurts to think about.

When I don't accept her offered glass, she gives me a perplexed look. "What is it?"

"It's part of what Tyler told me. That my parents died in a drunk driving accident. It was his parents who were drunk that night. It's why he doesn't drink...and why I don't think I want to for a while, anyway."

She sets the bottle and full glasses aside. "Of course, I'm so sorry. Your dopes of brothers didn't give me any details, only that you were having a rough time and that if you didn't answer my calls soon, then I should come to your house and camp out until you let me in."

I snort. And then the tears flow. They pour down my face, and she tugs me into her arms and holds me through the heavy wracking sobs taking hold of me again as my grief flashes to the forefront.

When it's over she asks gently, "Have you spoken to him? I know this might be hard to hear, but it's not his fault. The lying, yes, absolutely, but the fact that his parents killed yours. He was just as much a kid as you were."

"I know." I sniffle and wipe my face on the hem of my t-shirt. "I know it's not his fault. It's more like I can't face him with this history between us. It feels too big to get across."

"But it's not. You don't even have to make the effort. Just answer the phone the next time he calls. He'll likely do all the talking, and it'll be a gentle first step. I know you love him, and judging by how many times he's come here trying to get me to go talk to you, I think he loves you, too."

Another sniffle and snort. "But how? It hasn't been long enough, right?"

She gently tucks a wayward strand of hair behind my ears. Little pieces that have fallen out of the messy bun. "Since when does love have a timeline?"

I shake my head. "You're stupidly wise, you know that?"

"Duh." She grabs the wine and takes it to the kitchen. "I'll make some tea."

While she's in there, my phone rings, and it's Tyler's beautiful smiling face staring at me from the screen. I snapped the photo when we went hiking. The sun gleams off his skin, and he looks so happy to just be with me. Another wave of sadness crashes through me. I spend too much time staring and fumble to answer the phone.

Tyler's deep voice cuts through the line immediately, "Millie?"

"Yes?"

"You answered."

"So I did. What did you need?"

He huffs into the receiver like he hoped for a different response. I might be ready to talk to him, but I'm not sure I'm ready to forgive him...yet.

After a minute, he clears his throat and continues. "Uh, I know it's a bad time, but there are some people who wanted to meet you. And it's kind of important. Can you come to the studio? Just for a minute. You don't even have to talk to me if you don't want to."

That's the thing, I do want to see him and I hate that he has that much hold over me. "Who wants to meet me?"

"A record company."

My stomach pitches. I'm unable to digest the words. "What?"

"Yeah, they were there that night we sang together. They

love your voice and they'd like to talk to you." There's a pause, then he adds. "Millie, this isn't about us. This is your chance for the world to discover your talent. I don't even care if they just sign you. Please come meet them."

"It's not that I don't want to talk to you. I just can't yet."

"No, I get it. Are you coming?"

"Where are you?"

"At our studio in Rosewood."

Raising my chin, I suck in the emotion. "Okay."

"Great. See you in about forty minutes."

Before I can say anything he disconnects the call. Not quite sure how to react, I stare at the phone.

"Whatcha thinking?" Jess slides on the chair across from me. "You look deep in thought."

I quickly tell her about the phone call and what it all means. Before I know it she's on her feet, enveloping me into a massive hug.

"Go meet them," she encourages. "If you don't, you'll always wonder. This is your chance, Millie."

"I love you."

"Of course you do," she says as she taps something on her phone. "I called you a Lyft. The driver is outside. Call me later."

Heart racing, I rush to the car service and head off to Rosewood. I'm still unsure what I'm going to do. All I know is the faster I get this over with, the faster I can get away from people. Let my emotions settle back down again.

The door is open when I arrive, so I walk in to find a round man and a tall thin woman in business attire talking to Cash.

At the sound of my entrance, everyone turns to me. I'm suddenly fidgety, my hands wanting to smooth my still drying hair.

The man and woman step up first. She offers her hand and shakes mine. "Hi! My name is Talia. This is Henry. We're from Capital City Management. You have no idea how happy we are to meet you! I just know we are going to work on some incredible projects together!"

I stare between them. The man nods, agreeing with what she says. "Projects?" I stammer.

"I'm not going to lie to you," Henry says, "we love your voice and we love Devil's sound. We would love to sign you all as a band."

"What if she doesn't want to join the band?" Tyler asks.

Henry shrugs. "It's all or nothing."

I glance around the room at Tyler and the other members of the band. My soul feels wafer thin. The fate of Tyler's band is up to me. A part of me wants to run away. I'm a big girl. I've been through tougher times. This is also a chance for me to follow my dreams. Music is my genesis and forever my destination.

But can I say yes to my adventure and work alongside Tyler?

TYLER APPROACHES and leads me to a small room. "I was hoping they would offer you a contract. I didn't realize it was all of us together or nothing."

"If I say no?"

"Then you say no." He pauses then adds, " We want you to join the band."

Being so close to him starts a war inside me. Everything in me tingles to touch him, to run my fingers up his long neck and breathe him in. But my brain reminds me of the lies.

Tears choke my throat, burning as they threaten to

bubble and spill from my eyes. I bite my bottom lip and swallow them back. "You and me..."

He takes a step closer to me and cups my face. Warm breath caresses my lips as he leans even closer, his nose brushing against mine.

"Millie."

I look up at him. Slowly, so slowly, he brings his lips down to mine for one too-short second. My body trembles like a leaf. My treacherous heart leaps, going a mile a minute. He's so close, so real. He hurt me. I'm mad at him. I miss him. I...I love him.

I plant my hands on his chest and establish some distance between us.

"Millie."

"No, Tyler. I can't." I step away from him and flee the room. Cash tries to intercept me before I get to the door, but I skirt him easily and rush out to the sidewalk.

Instead of calling a car, I walk, and I walk, not even sure where I'm headed until I finally tap on my phone for a car service. It's not until I reach out and touch the cool granite of my parent's gravestone that I realize where I am.

Among the trees, the wind whispers. I sink to the soft earth and trace their names with my fingers like I used to do as a child. I remember singing along with my mom, our favorite song. She would start the first line with her beautiful voice, and then I would sing the second line, trying to match the way the words rolled effortlessly from her mouth and without any break or coarse sound in her voice. Then my dad would walk in and hug us, singing along. My brothers sang too, but not the way I did.

I remember having breakfast at a dining table and struggling to get to the toast on the other side. My dad would pass it to me, but not before taking a bite first, just to make sure it was healthy and good enough for his princess. I remember so much yet so little.

I remember when David, my oldest brother, left us, and Mom pretended not to be hurt by him leaving. She showed care by asking different questions. The question I remember most is, "Did you take everything you need?"

From that moment, I always wanted to leave my town and have Mom and Dad wave me goodbye as I went on tour, following the wind. It was my dream. But it all came crashing down when they died. I was only eleven years old.

There are a lot of fond and happy moments with my parents that have stayed with me, but I don't seem to remember the accident or what happened. It is just a blur of a moment that feels like a dream, and no one ever really gave me information even though I asked. After a while, I stopped asking. Maybe it hurt my brothers then to tell me, or it brought bad memories.

Grief flows through me, and tears come in generous streams. I miss my parents. I wish they were here to provide guidance.

"What do I do, Mom? Dad? How can I get through this? It feels like there's this hole in my chest, and now someone's dropped a match inside. How do I put out this flame and carry on with my life?"

Of course, no one answers. The only person who can make these choices is me. But it feels good to be with them. To press my fevered skin to the cool stone of their marker. To feel, for just a moment, like they're listening and loving me through it.

18

TYLER

I think the first three days of her absence are difficult. Another five feels hard enough to break me. I'm dizzy with the need to see her, touch her, explain for the thousandth time to her face, and not inside my head.

But if I push her too hard, I could lose her. I fear that most of all. So I wait, and I wait. It's the hardest thing I've had to do. The band is frustrated with my lack of focus, even Gramps appears a bit annoyed with me.

I send her a text message. One message a day is all I allow myself. Anything more, and I'll devolve to a place I can't come back from.

Day 1:

Me: *You're always on my mind.*

Millie:

Day 2:

Me: *We should talk.*

Millie:

Day 3:

Me: *I'm sorry.*

Three squiggly dots appear and my heart races with hope. Then they disappear.

I even got the number to the hardware store and called her brother Rueben. Once he realized who it was, he hung up on me. But it helps to tell me she's not back at work yet. And then I don't feel like I'm any better than her overprotective brothers.

The band is in the studio, each of us considering the contract, but mostly everyone waiting to hear what Millie wants to do. No one resents the situation anymore, not when we all know she makes our sound into something deeper, something more.

Two hours after we descend on the studio, Coby slams one of her sticks down on a cymbal. The noise makes us all jump.

"Fuck, Coby," I mutter.

She glares at me and points one of her drumsticks at my face. "Why are you sitting here wallowing? Go to that girl's apartment, and make things right. Even if you can't, apologize again, and keep doing it until she's heard it so many times, she believes it."

"I don't want her to feel like I'm crowding her and trying to influence her decision."

"And texting her every day isn't crowding her?" Cash asks.

"That's more like stalking," Gavin chimes in.

I flip them the bird.

Coby crosses the room to where I'm sitting on a stool. "Go to her and get an answer about what the fuck she's doing."

"Watch it, Coby," I warn.

"If you guys were on speaking terms, you wouldn't hesitate to use your dick to lure her into agreeing, not when you know it's the right thing for us, and the right thing for her."

"Shit, Coby," Cash says. "You're going too far."

But neither of us looks at him. I scowl, but it stopped fazing her a long time ago. "Thinking I know what's best for her is what got me into this mess in the first place. I doubt she'll be too happy if I demonstrate I haven't learned my lesson."

"That's not what this is. You going to her, explaining, apologizing, isn't you thinking you know what's best. It's fighting for her. Every girl wants a man who will fight for her." A new sadness enters her eyes and like the fight's fizzled out of her, she plops back onto her stool.

"I've tried."

"You're sending her text messages. Man up." It's Gavin who speaks up from his lopsided chair. "Beg, grovel, tell her you're sorry, and if she gives you another chance you'll do better, you'll be better, for her."

Everyone stares at the quiet member of our group. The one who shies away from emotions like sunlight in high summer.

"What if she doesn't believe me?"

Coby turns back to me with one lingering look at Gavin. "Then you repeat yourself until she listens. She hasn't told you never to darken her doorstep again. Until that happens, keep trying, because she wants you to. And when she's ready to accept you back, she will."

Cash strums his guitar, sending a mellow note through the room. "Women are so confusing."

"Only to idiots with zero emotional intelligence," Coby grumbles. "We aren't difficult to figure out. Feed us, fuck us, and don't piss us off. Easy peasy."

"But this is so much more than that. I..." There's no need

to explain. Every member of my band knows what I've been fighting against.

"Then say it to her, not to me, or to us." Coby waves her hands around the room. "Talk to *her* about it. She's worth fighting for, right? This isn't about the contract, or the band, it's about both of you deserving to be happy."

"Who knew you had such a soft side," Gavin chides her.

She flicks him the middle finger.

"I'm not just hesitating because of her. I've spent my entire life feeling guilty about the people who died because of my parents. Now, I've got names and faces to go with and the guilt."

"I'm sure they know it wasn't your fault. None of it was your fault," Coby whispers softly.

"It's not just that." I suck in a breath and say the one thing I've been dying to say since I found out the truth. "I'm glad my parents aren't here to hurt anyone else."

Coby points to the door, her lone stick in hand. "Then say that to her."

I don't hesitate any longer. The drive to her apartment feels so much farther than I remember.

When I arrive, I hear voices through the door, low and insistent. But I don't want to get caught on the landing, so I knock.

She answers, and the sight of her sucks all the air from my lungs and replaces it with tar. I can barely breathe looking at her. "Hi," I manage.

"You're here."

God, that voice. Her face. I miss her so much. Before she can continue, I pull her into my arms and wrap her in a hug. Even if it's the last one before she shoves me down the stairs, it's worth it.

"I have something to say. Please, let me get it out." My

heart is a jackhammer behind my ribs, pounding too fast. "My parents used to hit me when they'd get drunk. When I first found out they died, I was....relieved. Then I felt guilty for feeling that way. But my parents were awful people who hurt me regularly. I'm happy they're dead, but I'm so sorry they took your happiness with them."

She shudders in my arms, and I squeeze her tighter, remembering the feel of her against my body. Someone clears their throat, and I glance up to find David and Rueben glaring at me.

She peels herself away from my chest and leads me across the room to sit beside her on the couch.

It hadn't been that easy, right? Not by the deep tension floating through the space.

Once she's sitting again, her feet tucked under her on the couch, she turns to her brothers. "As I was saying...I think I'm being given an opportunity that I can't turn down. It feels right to me, any other option feels like a failure."

"But, how do you know it will work out? That you won't come back here in a week or a month with your tail between your legs?" Rueben asks her, ignoring me.

Hope flares bright in my chest, but I keep it tamped down until she's finished making her case.

"I don't know that. But what I know is that if I do come back, having completely ruined all my chances in Nashville, Cherry Falls will be here. You'll be here. And that you love me, and you'll help me to the best of your ability while I start over. Am I right?"

"Well, yes..." David begins.

"And you know, deep down, that if you don't let me do this, then you're going to lose me, and I'll never be able to trust you again. I'm an adult now, I don't need you to protect me from the hard stuff," she says, her eyes catching mine, including me in that speech.

I give her the barest of nods.

"And you?" Rueben says to me. "What do you have to say about this?"

"I say she deserves this chance. She's so good, better than you think, or you wouldn't be fighting so hard against what needs to happen. She's going to be a star, and she'll make you proud to have raised her. As for anything else? I love her more than anything. If she forgives me and lets me do that, it's all I can ask for."

I can barely breathe through the hope, the joy, everything clogging my chest, displacing the black mood I'd been in for days.

Rueben and David stand up together and survey us, then she steps forward and lets them wrap her in a hug.

Rueben eyes me over her shoulder. "If anything, anything at all, happens to her, we'll be on the first ride out to Nashville and there won't be anywhere you can hide from us. I don't even care if it's a fucking paper-cut."

Millie pulls back and swats at his arm. "Okay, get out you two. I need to talk to him for a minute."

David calls from the door as she bodily shoves them through it. "This doesn't mean we like you."

Once she locks the door, she faces me. "I'm sorry I took so long to figure things out. I was mad at you for lying, not for what happened to my parents, I know that wasn't your fault."

My chest feels like someone kicked it hard. "I understand. I shouldn't have lied. My only excuse is I was so scared of losing you."

"I know. My brothers and I talked about it. They knew it

too and were tired of me moping around. Sometimes it takes me a couple days to process things. So, Nashville, huh?"

I pull her into my arms and tuck her against my chest. "Only if you want to."

"But your band. You won't have a contract without me."

"Only if you want to," I repeat. "I love you. I'll..." I swallow heavily. "I'll stay here with you if you don't want to go."

She jerks back and stares up at me, her eyes bright. "You'd give up your dreams for me."

"You're my dream now, Millie. Don't you see that?"

Instead of answering, she kisses me hard, pulling my mouth into hers to nip at my bottom lip. "I would never ask you to do that. Let's go to Nashville. Together."

19

MILLIE

Tyler and I don't get nearly enough time to make up, but a week later, I have my first official band practice. The record executives are excited to have us on board and want us moved to Nashville immediately so we can start recording. I've been working on packing up my apartment and helping my brother find a replacement to work in the store.

The day of band practice, I show up at the studio. Inside, the band is staring around the space, which has mostly been cleared out save the instruments and a table in the middle of the room. Silver confetti covers everything, and silver balloons hang down from the ceiling.

"Who did all this?" I ask as I close the door behind me.

Tyler pulls me into his arms immediately, and I savor the feel of them around me.

"The record company must have. To celebrate signing the contract. It's there on the table waiting for us."

I march over and stare down at the multi-page document. It's a fearsome thing, stacked neatly with tabbed sides where each of us is meant to sign.

A row of black pens line the edge of the document. I pick one up and hand it to Tyler. "What are you waiting for? Our newly signed agent approved the paperwork last week. You should do the honors."

A grin splits his face before he leans down, finds a tab with his initials on it and scribbles an illegible signature. Coby follows suit, then Cash, then Gavin, and finally…

My hand shakes as I extend it and scribble my name on a line. When I put the pen down, I wonder if I'm supposed to feel differently now. Somehow, in a short time I'd realized a dream I'd been harboring all my life, without even much effort.

The absurdity of it forces a bark of laughter through me, and it echoes in the empty space.

They all stare at me like I've lost my mind. "Sorry, I'm just waiting for the bubble to pop. I can't believe this is all happening, and it's real."

Cash brings out a bottle of champagne and sparkling grape juice for us. I decline the alcohol and share the juice with Tyler instead.

"To Devil on the Highway," Coby proposes. "Let's kick Nashville's ass!"

We click our flutes together and tip glasses to our lips. Our little party is stuffed with joy, and I can't believe this is my life now.

None of it feels real, not the silky tart juice as it goes down my throat, nor the fizzle kiss Tyler shares with me afterward where I can taste it on his tongue.

The band wanders away, not wanting to witness us making out, I'm sure. Tyler leads me to a corner to kiss me, but when he stops, I whine. "What?"

"I wanted to tell you I found a place for us in Nashville already. You can look at it and decide once we get there, but

I didn't want you, or your brothers, to worry about sleeping in a hotel room until we figured out lodgings."

I shake my head, tears already brimming. "No, I'm sure whatever you picked is lovely. That was thoughtful of you. My brothers will definitely appreciate a set address for my whereabouts when we arrive."

When I lean in to kiss him again, he dodges. "I also got Jess set up to come visit when she wants. It'll be busy the first few months, but I know you'll miss her and she, you."

"Come on, are you trying to make me cry right now? Shut up and kiss me."

But before we can do much of anything, the studio door opens, and my brothers storm in. Their big forms always seem to swallow up spaces when they arrive together.

Coby squares off with David at the door. It's almost comical with their height differences. "Can I help you?"

He points to me in the corner. "I'm here to see my sister for a moment."

She narrows her eyes and then nods once.

Tyler, knowing we are done kissing for now, leads me over to their sides.

"I'd like a moment alone with her," David tells him.

I gently nudge him toward his friends. "Don't worry, I'm too big to kidnap."

Tyler presses my palm to his lips and joins the band while Rueben comes around to take his place. Then David hands me a wrapped package.

"What is this?" I ask, taking it and ripping into the clumsy packaging.

Inside is my favorite brand of syrup, a locally bottled make from the forests just outside of town. "Oh, this is sweet. Thank you."

"If you need my French toast recipe when you get out

there, let me know. I'll send it to your boyfriend; he can cook it for you."

I laugh at the idea of domesticating Tyler. But the thought shoots an unexpected wave of lust through me. I need to get that man in an apron, STAT.

Rueben pulls me into a hug, and David follows. "We're going to miss you."

I nod between them. "I know, I'll miss you both, too."

When they pull out of my arms, Rueben circles behind me and lays something over my neck. I glance down to find a silver locket with flowers etched in the front. Inside, the oval pictures are of Mom and Dad, and one of David and Rueben we took ages ago when we went camping.

"It's beautiful," I whisper, tears pouring down my face now.

"It was Mom's. I kept it for you. I was going to give it to you on your wedding day, but I want you to have something of hers before you leave."

I nod and hug them both again, tighter this time. After I wipe my face on my sleeve, I point to the champagne. "Do you guys want to stay? Join the little party we've got going on here? We just signed the contracts."

They decline, give me one last hug and kiss on the cheeks, and then they're gone.

My heart clenches. This is the trouble with wanting and dreaming. Saying yes to something means saying no to something else. Saying no to something means saying yes to something else. I'm leaving Cherry Falls. I'm walking away from my brothers. I've never been away from them more than a night or two. According to the record company's schedule, I won't see them for at least six months once we get to Nashville.

Tyler is at my side immediately. "Are you alright? You looked sick there for a moment."

I shake my head. "No, it's nothing. I was just thinking. I've never been away from them for long before."

He kisses my forehead and whispers. "Let's get out of here."

I meet his eyes. They're dark, and the look in them shoots shivers through me. The whisper comes out before I even think. "Let's go."

We sneak out, and Tyler takes me back to his apartment. The door is barely closed before he's on me, stripping my shirt over my head and tossing it onto a box.

"There are so many things to do," I complain, but I'm jerking at his belt buckle despite my words.

"So many things," he says into the column of my neck. My bra falls loose, and I shift it off to join my growing pile of discarded clothing.

He takes my breasts in hand, one in each, and squeezes them gently. "I've been thinking about you in my bed for days now."

I nod, my throat tight. He shucks his pants and t-shirt quickly, and I step out of my jeans.

He leads me to his bed, which still has sheets on it thankfully, and lays me down on top. I shake my head and pull him toward me and urge him to lie down. When he settles with a grin, I straddle his lap and lean down to kiss him.

The humor is gone as he runs his hands over the curve of my ass. It feels so good, and I moan when he drags me down to press against the hard length of him.

Sparks fly and my heart lights up like fireworks. Shit. It's too much. Too much pleasure. Too much torture. Too much goodness.

I kiss him hard. He tastes like grape juice, and when I nudge him open with my tongue, he lets out a little growl that sizzles through me to my core.

I missed him, everything about him, and this. I missed kissing him. I try to take control, but I'm already rubbing against him, needing more. He grips the back of my head and flips me onto my back. His weight settling over me.

"Please," I say.

"Don't worry. I'm going to make you feel good," he whispers, his fingers dancing down my stomach to my core. Quickly, he drags my panties off my legs, resettles beside me, and finds my clit with his fingers. I arch into his touch and twine my hands in the sheets, seeking something to hold on to. To keep me anchored to the Earth.

He swirls his fingers slowly, teasingly over my core. I drop my head to the mattress and groan.

God, he's beautiful. His skin smooth and soft, his muscles long and lean as I take him in. It hits me all over again, he's mine. Every sexy inch of him.

"Come here," I say, and reach for him. First, he climbs off the bed, strips his underwear, and grabs a condom from under the mattress.

At my questioning look, he shrugs, sheepishly. "I was hoping." Then he slips the condom on.

He doesn't hesitate to come into my arms. I wrap myself around him, hands, thighs, and press my lips to his. He melts into me, aligning his cock at my core, the tip of him grazing my clit, and I shiver in anticipation.

He moans into my lips, grazing his mouth against mine, over my chin, and down my neck. I'm more than ready for him, so I reach between us to grip him. His hips jerk until he maneuvers to align at my pussy. Carefully, he slides into me.

There's no pain this time, only a stretching fullness I

want more of. He braces his weight on his forearms, keeping some of his heaviness on my body, and I love the feel of him over me.

"I love you," he whispers against my lips.

His words slip inside me as surely as his body does.

I savor them as much as I do every inch of him. "I love you, too."

He responds by arching his hips back and slides into me until every millimeter is buried deep inside, filling me all the way.

Home. Tyler is my home.

I gasp and scream his name.

My breath rushes out of me. My nerve endings come alive. Pleasure sizzles through my nerves, from my fingers to my toes.

Then he shifts my thighs up around his hips. "Give yourself to me, Millie. All of you."

"I'm yours." I raise my ass and hand myself over to him.

He cradles my hips and then he's thrusting inside me, deep and borderline rough, using each downstroke to drag the base of his cock against my clit.

My head spins. He kisses me hard and then pulls back to look at me before kissing me again.

And then again.

Each time harder, and rougher, tongue delving into my mouth as he moves faster. Each thrust deeper and harder, hips grinding in a punishing pace.

"Look at me," he commands. "Don't close your eyes."

I do as he says and a smile touches his lips.

"I want to watch you come, my sweet Millie."

A garbled moan breaks out of my mouth before I can steal it back. The exquisite friction sends me flying. My body clenches, and shatters, sensations rolling through me in a sinful chaos of bliss.

I throw my head back and cry out in pleasure, spasms rocking my body in tight, sensual waves. It takes seconds for my orgasm to build. I'm shaking with it when he increases his pace, panting along with me.

"Millie," he grunts my name, burying his head in my shoulder. With two quick thrusts, he comes as the last tremors ripple through me.

We stay still for a few seconds, then he's kissing me, a deep kiss with tongue and teeth.

When he comes up for air, I take in a deep breath of my own. A laugh follows as he rolls to his side and drags me along with him. I nestle against him, savoring the feel of him in this new way.

"Let's just stay like this until we have to leave," I whisper.

"Deal," he says.

We have packing to do and goodbyes to make. But this time is ours, and we keep it for ourselves.

EPILOGUE
TYLER

Eighteen Months Later

I can't believe we're back in Cherry Falls. Millie is in the passenger seat with a blindfold on her face. Our friends and family are standing beyond the driveway in the yard, and I wave at them to shut up as I come around the vehicle and help her out.

Carefully, I lead her from the car and walk her up the little brick sidewalk to the door. Her brothers, the band, Gramps, Jess, all mill about, excitement heavy in the air.

My hands are shaking with nerves which I hope she doesn't feel.

When we get to the door, I turn her to face me and press the key into her palm.

She rolls it in her hand. "What's this?"

"Remember how we talked about getting a place in Cherry Falls so we can spend more time there?"

She laughs. "Yeah."

"Well…" I snatch the blindfold from her face, and she jerks back from the door, not expecting it to be there.

Brows up, she asks, "You bought a house?"

It's my turn to laugh, and I tug her in close for a hug. Her smile enough to ease some of the tension in me. "Technically, we bought a house. I hope you're not upset. You said you loved the listing when you looked at it. I wanted to surprise you."

She shakes her head. "No. I'm not mad."

Then she realizes we aren't alone, and everyone yells, "Surprise!"

Momentarily, the new house is forgotten, and she rushes to grab everyone up in crushing hugs. We come home every few months, so it hasn't been that long since she's seen everyone.

She kisses Gramps' weathered cheeks and then turns back to the door. "Let's go in, then."

The door opens soundlessly, and she leads us all inside. It's not a huge house, but we both decided, even if our careers take off and we have more money than we could ever need, that we didn't want to live excessively. A modest house with just enough room to grow suits us fine.

She explores, as does everyone else—taking in the freshly painted walls and the dark wood furniture Jess picked out for us. Within reason and budget, I let her have free rein over the design, and she perfectly tailored the place in soft soothing grays and dark brown woods.

The backyard is decorated and food laid out for a party, so we converge on the little patio. A fence runs the perimeter of the property to give us privacy, and Cash takes up the grill as soon as we get outside.

Jess pours champagne for everyone who wants it and sparkling grape juice for me and Millie.

My heart thunders in my chest as she takes her glass and sips it. Then her eyes snag on the giant ring shaped pieces of ice inside it. I'm already on my knees when she turns back to me.

She gasps, and Coby lets out a little squeal of excitement behind me. I'm laughing as I tug the black ring box from my pocket, open it, and hold it up to her.

"I know it's been a whirlwind between us, Millie. But almost immediately after I met you, I knew I wanted to spend the rest of my life making you smile. The rest of my life making music with you. And the rest of my life savoring every second we spend together. Will you be my wife?"

She nods as she throws herself at me, completely ignoring the ring in my still outstretched hand. I squeeze her tight against me and stand up. Once she kisses me senseless, she pulls back to look at the ring.

This is courtesy of her brothers. A beautiful cushion cut diamond which belonged to her mother, and her grandmother before her. Tears sheen her eyes as I slip the ring on her, and she admires it in the light.

She looks around at everyone and whispers, "Thank you."

Her brothers grab her up in bone crunching hugs first. Then the rest of the band oohs and ahhs over the sparkling piece of jewelry.

"You've given me a gift," she tells me, when I finally get her back by my side. "I have one for you too."

"Me? All I need is you."

She laughs and digs a piece of paper out of her pocket. With a trembling hand, she wraps my fingers around it.

My brain takes a minute to catch up to what I'm seeing. And then I'm the one crying, sinking to my knees on the concrete patio all over again. A heavy weight has entered my chest and I can barely breathe around it.

I'm going to be a father. A father.

She follows me down and clutches my head to her belly. I turn and press a kiss to it, holding her tight around the hips. My tears mar her shirt, but she doesn't seem to care, and neither do I.

"What?" David asks. "Your album went multiplatinum and won record of the year. Congrats on the success by the way, but what's happening now?"

Jess claps and jumps up and down beside him. "You're going to be an uncle, you big idiot."

He glares at her but then catches up and stares at us slack-jawed. "An uncle?"

Rueben steps up beside him, surveying us, a heavy look in his eyes. "Do you know when?"

She shakes her head. Still grinning ear to ear. "In the winter, so get ready."

I stand again and clutch her tight to my chest. "You make me so happy," I whisper just for her.

"You make me happy, too."

I nod and lead her to sit at the picnic table on our new patio. Alone from everyone, I look up into Millie's green eyes, feeling the love she has for me unfold me. I don't know what I ever did to deserve her, but I plan on spending the rest of my life proving to her I'm worth it. If I spend the rest of my life ensuring she stays happy, it won't be long enough.

THE END

330 LOVE LN. PLAYLIST

330 Love Ln. Playlist

Love Story– Taylor Swift

Everything I wanted – Billie Ellish

Jolene – Dolly Parton

Dust to Dust – The Civil Wars

Adore You – Harry Styles

This is Me Trying – Taylor Swift

Till Forever – Joy Williams

I Was Born to Love You – Ray LaMontagne

ACKNOWLEDGMENTS

Big hugs to my beta readers for your patience and your sage words. Thank you to Cormar Covers for the gorgeous cover! My editor and proofreader for your brilliance. Huge gratitude to all the bloggers who continue to participate in my journey. Love to all of my readers. Without you, this ride wouldn't be as much fun. A special shout out to my husband, you're sexier than any book boyfriend. Thank you for all of your support and our Happy Chaos.

ABOUT THE AUTHOR

Mika Jolie lives in New Jersey with her Happy Chaos—her husband and their energizer bunnies. She's a lover of words, wonder, an old-fashioned, and the whimsical delights of everyday living. When she's not writing swoon-worthy, sexy relatable romance, you can find her on a hiking adventure, beachin' it at the Jersey shore, apple, blueberry picking, or whatever her three men can conjure up.

She loves to hear from readers. Connect with Mika on BookBub, her reader group Mika Jolie's Wildflowers, Facebook, Amazon, Instagram and Goodreads.

BookBub | **Mika Jolie's Wildflowers** | **Facebook** | **Amazon** | **Instagram** | **Goodreads**

ALSO BY MIKA JOLIE

MARTHA'S WAY SERIES

The Scale

Need You Now

Tattooed Hearts

Wrapped in Red

In Between Forever

PLATONICALLY COMPLICATED

The Boy Friend

Explicitly Yours

Rules of Engagement

The Player – Coming May 2021

Add to Your TBR

PLAYING FOR KEEPS

Intercepted Hearts

Defenseless Hearts

VEGAS IS CALLING SERIES

Paging Dr. Hook Up

What Happened in Vegas

STANDALONE NOVELS

Somewhere to Begin

Layla's Chance

One Complicated Christmas

Home for Christmas

Hometown Sweetheart

Irresistibly Irish

COMING IN 2021

Sex, Lust, Love, Hate – Coming April 2021

Add to Your TBR

713 Main Street – A Cherry Falls Romance – Coming July 13th

Add to Your TBR